The Hatter's Phantoms
GEORGES SIMENON

Translated from the French by Willard R. Trask

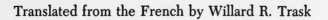

The Hatter's

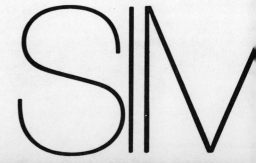

Helen and Kurt Wolff Book   Harcourt Brace Jovanovich   New York and London

Phantoms

Library of Congress Cataloging in Publication Data

Simenon, Georges, 1903-
The hatter's phantoms.

Translation of Les fantômes du chapelier.
"A Helen and Kurt Wolff book."
I.   Title.
PZ3.S5892Hat   [PQ2637.I53]   843'.9'12   76-18254
ISBN 0-15-139270-6

First edition

B C D E

The Hatter's Phantoms
GEORGES SIMENON

It was December 3, and still raining. The figure 3 stood out, very big and black, with a sort of fat belly, against the staring white of the calendar which hung, just to the right of the till, against the dark oak partition between the salesroom and the show window. It was exactly three weeks ago, for it had been on November 13 (another fat 3 on the calendar) that the first old woman had been murdered, near the church of Saint-Sauveur, a few steps from the canal.

Yes, it had been raining since November 13. You could almost say that during those three weeks it had rained without ever stopping.

Most of the time it was a steady, spattering rain, and when you went about the town, sticking close to the houses, you heard the water running in the gutter pipes; you chose the streets with arcades, to be sheltered if only for a moment; you changed your shoes when you got home; in every house hats and overcoats hung drying near the stove, and people who didn't have a change of clothes lived in a perpetual cold dampness.

It got dark well before four o'clock, and some windows were lighted all day long.

It was four o'clock when, as on every afternoon, Monsieur Labbé had left the back room (known as the workroom), where wooden heads of all sizes stood in rows on the shelves. He had gone up the spiral staircase at the far end of the room. On the landing, he had stopped for a moment, taken a key from his pocket, opened the door of the bedroom, preparatory to turning on the light.

But before flicking the switch, had he gone to the window, whose lace curtains—very thick and dusty— were always closed? Probably, for he normally let down the blind before turning on the light.

At that moment he had been able to see, across the street and only a few yards away from him, Kachoudas, the tailor, in his workroom. It was so close, the gap made by the street was so narrow, that you had the feeling you were living in the same house.

Kachoudas' workroom, which was on the second floor, above his shop, had no curtains. The smallest details of the room stood out as in an engraving—the flowery design of the wallpaper, the fly specks on the mirror, the thick flat piece of chalk hanging from a string, the brown-paper patterns pinned to the wall, and Kachoudas, sitting on his table, with his legs crossed under him and, within reach of his hand, an unshaded electric-light bulb, which he brought close to his work by a length of wire. The door at the back, which gave onto the kitchen, was always part way open, but usually not enough for the inside of the kitchen to be visible. Yet Madame Kachoudas' presence made itself felt, for from time to time her husband's lips moved. They talked to each other, from room to room, while they worked.

Monsieur Labbé had talked too; Valentin, his assistant, who stayed downstairs in the salesroom, had heard a murmur of voices, footsteps over his head. Then he had seen the hatter come down again, first his elegantly shod feet, his trousers, his jacket, finally his face, with its rather indeterminate features, serious looking but never exaggeratedly so, never stern, the face of a man who is self-sufficient, who feels no need to put himself forward.

Before going out on that day Monsieur Labbé had steamed two more hats, one of them a gray felt that belonged to the mayor, and all the while he worked on

them there was the sound of the rain in the street, of the water pouring down the gutter pipe, and the faint hissing of the gas stove in the shop.

It was always too hot there. No sooner did he arrive in the morning than Valentin, the assistant, felt the blood go to his head, and by afternoon his head felt heavy; sometimes he saw his eyes, bright as if with fever, in the mirrors between the sets of shelves.

Monsieur Labbé talked no more than he did on other days. He could spend hours with his assistant and not say a word to him.

There were other sounds around them, but close by: the tick of the pendulum of the big clock, and at every quarter-hour the sound of a spring letting go. At the hours and half-hours the mechanism started into action, but after an ineffectual effort stopped short: the clock— or so it would seem—had originally had a set of chimes, which had got out of order.

If the little tailor could not see into the room on the second floor—by day because of the curtains, by night because of the blind—he had only to bend his head to see all the way into the hat shop.

He was certainly watching. Monsieur Labbé didn't take the trouble to make sure, but he knew it. It was no reason to make any change in his schedule. His movements remained slow and meticulous. He had very beautiful hands, a little pudgy, and amazingly white.

At five minutes before five he had left the workroom, putting out the light, and he had made one of his ritual remarks:

"I'll go see if Madame Labbé needs anything."

Again he had set out up the spiral staircase. Valentin had heard his footsteps on the floor above, a muffled murmur of voices, then had seen his feet again, his legs, his whole body. Monsieur Labbé had opened the door to the kitchen and had said to Louise:

"I shall be back early. Valentin will shut up the shop."

He said the same words every day, and the maid answered:

"Yes, sir."

Then, putting on his heavy black overcoat, he said the same thing over again to Valentin—who, of course, had already heard it.

"Yes, sir. Good night, sir."

"Good night, Valentin."

He took some money from the till and lingered a moment longer, looking at the windows across the street. He was sure that Kachoudas, who had seen his shadow a little earlier on the second-floor curtain, had come down from his table.

What was he saying to his wife? For he was saying something to her. He had to have an excuse. She asked him no questions. She would not have allowed herself to make a remark to him. For years now, at about five o'clock in the afternoon he would go to drink a glass or two of white wine at the Café des Colonnes. Monsieur Labbé went there too, as well as others, who didn't stop at white wine or at two glasses. For most of them it was the end of the workday. But when Kachoudas got home, he ate dinner hurriedly among his brood of small children and then climbed onto his table again, where he often remained working until eleven o'clock or midnight.

"I'm going out for a breath of air."

He was very much afraid that he would miss Monsieur Labbé. The latter had understood. It didn't date from the first old woman who had been murdered, but from the third, when the town was becoming really panic-stricken.

The Rue du Minage was almost always empty at that hour, especially when rain was coming down in torrents. It was emptier than ever now that people in general avoided going out after nightfall. The shopkeepers, who

had been the first to suffer from the panic, had also been the first to organize patrols. But had the patrols succeeded in preventing the deaths of Madame Geoffroy- Lambert and of Madame Léonide Proux, the midwife from Fétilly?

The little tailor was timid, and Monsieur Labbé indulged himself in the malicious pleasure of waiting for him without seeming to. Was it a diabolical pleasure, or not?

He finally opened his door—which made the shop bell ring. He passed under the enormous top hat made of red sheet metal that served as the sign of his establishment, turned up the collar of his overcoat, thrust his hands deep into his pockets. There was a bell on Kachoudas' door too, and after a few steps along the sidewalk Monsieur Labbé was sure to hear it.

It was a street with arcades, like most of the old streets in La Rochelle. So no rain fell on the sidewalks. They were like cold, damp tunnels, where there was light only at long intervals, with gateways that opened onto blackness.

On the way to the Place d'Armes, Kachoudas deliberately kept step with the hatter, but even then he was so afraid of an ambush that he chose to walk in the rain in the middle of the street.

As far as the corner they met no one. Then came the show windows of the perfumer's shop, the pharmacy, the haberdashery, and finally the wide bay windows of the café. Jeantet, the young newspaperman, with his long hair, his thin face, his burning eyes, was at his outpost at the first table near the window, writing his article in front of a cup of coffee.

Monsieur Labbé did not smile, did not appear to see him. He heard the little tailor's footsteps approaching. He turned the door handle, made his way into the pleasant warmth, moved at once to the center tables near the stove and between the columns, and stood

there behind the cardplayers while the waiter, Gabriel, relieved him of his overcoat and hat.

"How are you, Léon?"

"Pretty well."

They had all known each other too long—most of them ever since school—to want to converse. The ones who were playing cards gave a little nod or mechanically touched the newcomer's hand.

From force of habit Gabriel asked:

"The usual?"

And the hatter sat down, with a sigh of satisfaction, behind one of the bridge players, Dr. Chantreau, whom he called Paul. He had seen at a glance where the game stood. It could be said to have been going on for years, since it started again every day at the same hour, at the same table, with the same drinks in front of the same players, the same pipes, and the same cigars.

The central heating must have been inadequate, for Oscar, the proprietor, had kept the big shiny black stove, toward which Monsieur Labbé stretched his legs to dry his shoes and the bottoms of his trousers. The little tailor had had time to enter, to make his way to the central tables in his turn, but not with the same assurance; he had greeted the company respectfully, though no one answered him, and had sat down on a chair.

He did not belong to the group. He had not been to the same schools or the same barracks. At the age when the cardplayers were becoming bosom friends, he had lived God knows where in the Near East, where people of his kind were shipped like cattle from Armenia to Smyrna, from Smyrna to Syria, Greece, or somewhere else.

At first, some years earlier, he had sat down a little farther away to drink his white wine, followed the game, which he could not have known, with a sustained concentration that brought wrinkles to his forehead. Then, imperceptibly, he had made his way nearer, first mov-

ing his chair, then changing chairs, then openly changing tables, until he was directly behind the players.

No one said anything about the old women or the terror that dominated the city. It may have been discussed at other tables, but not at theirs. Laude, the senator, took his pipe from his mouth to ask, scarcely turning toward the hatter:

"Your wife?"

"Same as ever."

It had been a habit with his friends for the past fifteen years. Gabriel had served him his Picon with grenadine, dark mahogany in color, and he drank a mouthful of it slowly, glancing once at young Jeantet busy producing his article for the *Écho des Charentes*. A clock with its dial framed in a ring of copper hung between the café proper and the back of the establishment, where the billiard tables stood. It pointed to a quarter past five when Julien Lambert, the insurance agent, who was losing as usual, asked the hatter:

"Will you take my place?"

"Not this evening."

This was nothing out of the ordinary. There were six or seven of them who alternately played cards or sat behind the players. Only Kachoudas was never asked to play, and probably it was beyond the scope of his ambition.

He was short, puny. He smelled bad and he knew it; he knew it so well that he avoided getting too close to the others. It was a smell that belonged to him and his family, which could have been called the "Kachoudas smell," a mixture of the garlic they used in cooking and the grease of the woolen materials he made up. Here people said nothing, politely pretended not to notice it; but at school some of their more outspoken classmates would protest when they were made to sit beside the little Kachoudas girls.

"You stink! Your sister stinks! You all stink!"

He was smoking one of his few cigarettes of the day, for he couldn't smoke while he worked, for fear of burning his customers' clothes. He rolled his own cigarettes, and they always had a big stain of saliva on the end.

It was December 3, and quarter past five. It was raining. The streets were pitch dark. It was hot in the café, and Monsieur Labbé, the hatter from the Rue du Minage, watched the doctor, who had just bid five clubs, only to be rashly doubled by the insurance agent.

Tomorrow morning when they read the paper, they would all find out what young Jeantet was busy writing about the murdered old women, for he was conducting an impassioned investigation and had even in a way challenged the police.

His employer, the printer Jérôme Caillé, who also edited the paper, was quietly playing bridge without a thought for the hotheaded young man whose article he would glance over when he went back a little later.

Chantreau had his fingers on a trump and was about to risk the deciding finesse when out of the corner of his eye Monsieur Labbé saw Kachoudas half rise, but without entirely losing contact with his chair, lean toward him, and put out his hand as if to pick up something from the sawdust that covered the floor.

But it was at the hatter's trousers that he was aiming. His tailor's eye had noticed a little white speck near the cuff. Could he have thought it was anything but a bit of thread? He certainly harbored no evil intentions. Even if he had, he couldn't possibly have guessed the importance of his action.

No more did Monsieur Labbé, who did nothing to stop him, a little surprised but not in the least uneasy.

"Excuse me."

Kachoudas grasped the white object, which was not a

thread but a tiny bit of paper, scarcely a quarter of an inch long, rather thin and rough, like newsprint.

No one in the café paid the slightest attention to what was happening. Kachoudas was holding the scrap of paper between thumb and forefonger. It was certainly by chance that, his body leaning forward, his head bent, the tips of his buttocks still touching his chair, he glanced at it. But it wasn't just a bit of a newspaper. It had been carefully cut out with scissors. To be precise, two letters had been cut out, an *n* and a *t* at the end of a word.

Monsieur Labbé looked down, and the little tailor suddenly stopped moving, panic-stricken; then he finally raised his head, straightened up his body, and, avoiding looking the hatter in the eye, held the minute object out to him, stammering:

"I beg your pardon."

Instead of throwing the bit of paper away, he handed it over; and that was a mistake, for he thereby admitted that he had understood its importance. Because he was timid and knew that his lot in life was to be humble, he made a second mistake by beginning a sentence that he didn't have the courage to finish:

"I thought . . ."

He saw nothing except, in a luminous haze, chairs, people's backs, fabrics, sawdust on the floor, the black feet of the stove, and he heard a serious voice calmly saying:

"Thank you, Kachoudas."

For they were on speaking terms. Every morning at eight o'clock the hatter and the tailor would come out to take down the boards that served as shutters for their shops. The pork butcher's, next door to Kachoudas' shop, had already long been open. On Saturdays the farm women from the neighborhood who had vege-

tables or poultry to sell blocked the street with their baskets, but on other days only the paving stones separated the two men, and Kachoudas had got into the habit of saying:

"Good morning, Monsieur Labbé."

He would add, according to the weather:

"Fine day today."

Or:

"Still raining."

And the hatter would answer good-naturedly:

"Good morning, Kachoudas."

That was all. They were two shopkeepers whose shops faced each other.

This time he had just heard Monsieur Labbé say:

"Thank you, Kachoudas."

And it was in almost the same tone of voice. Could it have been exactly the same tone of voice, despite all the horror of the little tailor's discovery? Kachoudas wished he could swallow his whole glass of white wine at one gulp. The glass rattled against his teeth. He tried to think very quickly, very clearly, and the harder he tried, the more confused his thoughts became.

Above all, he mustn't turn his head to the right. He had decided on that the very first moment.

The men at the center table, where the senator, the printer, the doctor, the hatter sat, were from sixty to sixty-five years of age—in short, the most important patrons of the café; but at other tables there were other players, and, more particularly, to the right the pinochle players, who represented the generation of men of from forty to fifty. And at that table, almost every day from five to six o'clock, you could see Inspector Pigeac, the police detective charged with investigating the case of the old women.

At all costs, Kachoudas must keep from looking in his direction. Nor could he turn toward the young reporter, who was still writing. Was Jeantet busy, once again,

answering another message from the murderer? Probably.

In three weeks there had been time for it to become a habit, almost a tradition. After each murder the newspaper would receive a communication made up partly from individual letters, partly from entire words, cut from earlier issues of the *Écho des Charentes,* and the paper would publish it, followed by a commentary written by young Jeantet. The next day, or the day after that, the murderer would answer in his turn, always by means of bits of paper cut out and pasted onto a blank sheet.

As it happened, yesterday's message had contained a sentence that froze the little tailor to the marrow.

You are wrong, young man. I am not a coward. It is not from cowardice that I attack only old women, but out of necessity. If tomorrow I should find it equally necessary to attack a man, however big and strong, I would do it.

Some of the messages, half a column long, represented hundreds of patiently cut-out letters—which had inspired Jeantet to write:

Not only is the murderer patient and meticulous, but his life style leaves him with plenty of leisure.

The nineteen-year-old journalist—patient too, in his way—had made an experiment. He had worked out the time it would take to compose a message thirty lines long by means of letters cut out of old newspapers. Kachoudas did not remember the exact result, but it was staggering.

If tomorrow I should find it equally necessary to attack a man . . .

One of them was smoking his pipe in little puffs and watching the card game, the other had a dirty cigarette butt stuck to his lip and did not dare to let his eyes rest anywhere. From time to time Monsieur Labbé glanced at the clock, and it was only twenty-five past five when he ordered his second Picon. It was half past five when

he stood up—which was enough to bring Gabriel running with his overcoat and hat.

Did he really look Kachoudas over with ironic benevolence? There was a layer of smoke stretching just above the cardplayers' heads. The stove sent out puffs of heat. It really seemed that Monsieur Labbé was waiting, that he guessed exactly what the little tailor was thinking.

"If I let him leave by himself, he's quite capable of lying in wait for me somewhere in the dark along the Rue du Minage. . . ."

And what if Kachoudas spoke out now, no matter to whom, to the inspector or even the newspaperman? What if he announced, pointing his forefinger:

"He's the one!"

The bit of paper had vanished. Kachoudas couldn't see a sign of it. He remembered that the hatter had rolled it between his fingers, had made a grayish pill of it. And even if the two cut-out letters were still there on the floor? How could he prove he'd taken them from Monsieur Labbé's trousers?

Even that wouldn't be enough. Witness the fact that Monsieur Labbé hadn't even blinked, hadn't been frightened, had simply said:

"Thank you, Kachoudas."

And twenty thousand francs were at stake, a fortune for a little tailor whose customers scarcely ever entrusted him with anything more than mending a tear or turning a suit, and whose eldest daughter worked as a salesgirl at Prisunic.

If he wanted to earn the twenty thousand francs, he had to do better than simply make an unsupported accusation. He oughtn't to have put the murderer on his guard.

Now, Monsieur Labbé knew. And Monsieur Labbé, who had killed five old women since November 13— that is, in three weeks—could very easily get rid of *him.*

Did Kachoudas really have time to think of all that? The hatter was already touching fingertips with his friends. They were saying:

"Good night, Léon."

For his first name was Léon. He gave the doctor, who was dealing and so had both hands occupied, a pat on the shoulder, and the doctor muttered:

"I hope Mathilde will be getting better."

It really seemed that he was delaying purposely, to give Kachoudas time to make up his mind. The expression on his face was just the same as it had been an hour or so before, when Valentin had seen him coming down the spiral staircase. Earlier in his life he had been fat. He might even have been very fat, and then had partly melted away—you could tell it from his soft outlines, his indeterminate features. Even so, he must still weigh twice as much as Kachoudas.

"See you tomorrow."

The minute hand had just moved beyond the half-hour. Kachoudas quickly picked up his overcoat from the chair beside him. He almost left without paying, he was so afraid that Monsieur Labbé would have turned the corner of the Rue du Minage before he was out of the café himself. For, if that were so, every kind of ambush became possible. Yet he had to get home.

Monsieur Labbé walked on at his usual even pace, neither slow nor fast, and for the first time the little tailor noticed that, like most fat men or former fat men, he was extremely light on his feet and that he made no sound as he walked.

He turned right into the Rue du Minage. Kachoudas followed him, some twenty yards behind, carefully keeping to the middle of the street. He would always have time to shout in case of need. Two or three shops were still open; he saw their lights through the rain. Almost all the living quarters, on the upper floors, were lit up.

Monsieur Labbé stayed on the left-hand sidewalk, onto which the door of his shop opened, but instead of stopping there, he walked on and, a little farther along, turned his head, perhaps to make sure that his neighbor was still following him. He needn't have done so, for Kachoudas' footfalls were clattering along the pavement.

The little tailor could go home. The way was clear. His shop was still open and he would have time quickly to bolt the door. Through the second-floor window he saw the piece of chalk hanging over the table near the light bulb. The children were home from school. Esther, his eldest daughter, the one who worked at Prisunic, would come home a little after six o'clock—running, for she too was afraid of the murderer and none of her fellow salesgirls lived in the district.

He went on. He turned to the left like Monsieur Labbé, and for a little while they were in a more brightly lighted street. It was reassuring to see people in the shops, an occasional car driving past throwing up water from the puddles.

There were no more arcades, and Monsieur Labbé took the rain on his shoulders. The street became dark again. Now the hatter would disappear, now reappear in the circle of light from a street lamp, and Kachoudas stuck exactly to the middle of the street, holding his breath, numb with terror, yet unable to turn back.

How many groups of volunteers were patrolling the city at that hour? Probably four or five, with flashlights, counting the young men who did it for the fun of it. It was the fatal hour. Three of the old women had been murdered between half past five and seven in the evening.

One behind the other, they came to the quiet district around the museum, with little one-story houses; and behind some of the windows families could be seen

gathered together, children doing their homework, women already setting the table for dinner.

Suddenly Monsieur Labbé vanished into the darkness, and after a few steps Kachoudas stopped short, as if he had suddenly lost something essential: he couldn't place his neighbor because of the blackness that shrouded the street. Wouldn't he be waiting stock-still, drawn up in some corner? But then again, mightn't he be moving? Wasn't he able to move without making a sound? No—nothing proved that he wasn't closing in on the little tailor, and the little tailor stood there as if paralyzed by an arctic cold.

Not far away he heard the sound of a piano. A weak light filtered through the slatted blinds of a house. In a brightly lit room, a little girl, or a little boy, was taking a music lesson, tirelessly beginning the same scales over and over again.

Not a human being entered the street, from either one end or the other, and Monsieur Labbé was still hidden somewhere, silent, invisible, while Kachoudas did not dare approach any of the houses.

The piano stopped, and there was utter silence. Then came the dull sound of the cover being dropped over the black and white keys. Light on the other side of a house door, muffled voices becoming clearer as the door opened twenty yards from the little tailor, while the raindrops were transformed into sparks of light.

"You really insist, Mademoiselle Mollard? It would be so much safer to wait till my husband gets home from the office. He'll be here in ten minutes."

"For the little way I have to go! Do go back into the house now! You'll catch a cold. See you next Friday."

It was a Friday. It must be that the little girl (or little boy) took a piano lesson every Friday from five to six.

"I'll leave my door open until you're home."

"I won't hear of it! You'd just get the whole house cold. I tell you I'm not afraid."

From her voice, Kachoudas imagined she was small and thin, a trifle bent, a trifle overrefined. He heard her come down the steps, start along the sidewalk. The door, left open for a moment, was finally shut. He nearly cried out. He wanted to cry out. But it was already too late. In any case, he would have been physically incapable of it.

The thing made no more noise than, say, a pheasant flying out of a wood. It was probably the rustling of clothes. Everyone in the city knew how it was done, and despite himself Kachoudas raised his hand to his throat, imagined the cello string tightening around the victim's neck, made a determined effort to shake off his immobility.

He was sure it was over, and he must get away as quickly as possible, run to the police station. There was one in the Rue Saint-Yon, just beyond the market.

He thought he had spoken aloud, though his lips had simply been moving without making a sound. He was walking. It was a victory. He couldn't yet manage to run. In any case, mightn't it be better not to run, here, in these empty streets, where the other could run too, overtake him, finish him off as he had just finished the old lady off?

A show window. Ironically enough, it was a gunsmith's. To be sure, the hatter never used firearms. Kachoudas no longer felt so much alone. He could catch his breath. He would have liked to turn back. Another twenty yards, ten yards, and he'd see the red light of the police station.

He had stumbled through puddles, and his feet were soaked, his features stiff with cold. He was walking like a normal person again; he passed the Rue du Minage, his street.

He had almost made it. He didn't hear so much as a footfall, but he knew that someone was walking behind him, that he would be overtaken. He didn't dare start

running again, he didn't dare stop, and a silhouetted figure taller and bulkier than himself appeared to his left, footsteps fell into time with his own, and a strangely calm voice declared: "You'd be making a mistake, Kachoudas."

He didn't look toward his companion. He didn't answer. He didn't turn back right away.

He was alone. He saw the red lamp, a policeman leaving the station and getting onto his bicycle.

He turned around. Showing no further interest in him, Monsieur Labbé, who had turned on his heel too, was walking, with his hands in his pockets and his overcoat collar turned up, toward the Rue du Minage, toward their own street.

2

When he arrived in front of his shop shutters, which
Valentin had put up, he stopped, then unbuttoned his
overcoat to take his bunch of keys from his trousers
pocket. He had always gone through exactly the same
ritual when he got home in the evening. Someone had
stopped at the corner of the Rue du Minage. It was
Kachoudas, who was waiting for the hatter's door to be
closed before entering his own house.

Monsieur Labbé looked up and saw the tailor's wife in
the workroom on the second floor. Feeling a little
uneasy, she had come to look out the window.

He turned the key in the lock, made his way into the
warm darkness, closed the door before turning the electric-light switch, barred the door, then remained standing where he was, with his face pressed against a crack in
the shutter.

The little tailor, still keeping cautiously to the middle
of the street, finally arrived in front of his house. He
walked oddly, as if by jumps. Monsieur Labbé noticed
for the first time that he threw one leg out a little.
Kachoudas was looking up too, but his wife had just gone
back to the kitchen. He plunged headlong into his shop,
but he had to come out again to put up the shutters,
since he had no assistant to do it for him. All his movements were nervous, jerky. He must have called out,
turning to face the staircase (the same kind of spiral
staircase as the one at the hatter's):

"It's me!"

He hurried to shut the door and bolt it. The light on
the ground floor went out and a little later reappeared in

the workroom, where the little tailor's first concern was to go and look out the window.

Monsieur Labbé left his observation post, replaced what remained of the money he had taken from the till before leaving, went back into the workroom, and fiddled with an object that he took from his pocket and that looked like a toy put together by some street urchin—two pieces of wood connected by some sort of cord.

The table was set for one, with a white tablecloth and a bottle of wine that had been opened and then recorked with a silver stopper.

"Good evening, Louise. Has Madame called?"

"No, sir."

The maid looked at his feet as he sat down in front of the stove, then came back carrying a pair of slippers and knelt on the floor. He had never asked her to do this. She must have been taught at home on the farm to take off the men's shoes—her father's, her brothers'—when they came in from the fields.

It was as hot here as it was in the shop, and the air had the same stagnant weight that seemed to enclose objects as in a frame, gave them a look of being fixed for all eternity.

Beyond the window that looked out on the courtyard the rain could still be heard falling, and inside there was the sound of a very old clock in a walnut case, swinging a copper disk back and forth, more slowly, it really seemed, than anywhere else. The time it told was not the same as in the shop or as the time told by Monsieur Labbé's watch or by the alarm clock on the second floor.

"Has anyone called?"

"No, sir."

She put his fine patent-leather slippers on his feet.

The room was more a dining room than a kitchen, for the cooking stove and the sink were to one side, in a cramped alcove. The table was round, the chairs uphol-

stered in studded leather. There were many copper pots, and on a rustic sideboard old chinaware bought at the auction room.

"I'm going up to see if Madame needs anything."

"May I serve the soup?"

He vanished up the spiral staircase, and she heard the door on the second floor open, footsteps, murmuring, the sound of the casters as the armchair was pushed across the room as on every other evening. When he came downstairs again, he said, as he seated himself at the table:

"She's not very hungry. What is there for dinner?"

He had put his book in front of him, taken his tortoise-shell glasses from their case. The stove warmed his back. He ate slowly. Louise served him and between the courses waited motionless in her alcove, staring into space.

She had not yet reached twenty. She was rather fat, extremely stupid, with protuberant, expressionless eyes.

The cubbyhole that served as the kitchen was not big enough to hold a table. Sometimes she ate there standing, sometimes she waited for the hatter to finish and leave the room before she sat down at his place.

He disliked her. He'd made a poor bargain when he'd hired her, but there'd be plenty of time to think about that later on.

At a quarter to eight he wiped his mouth, put his rolled-up napkin into the silver ring, recorked the bottle, from which he had drunk only one glass, and stood up with a sigh.

"It's ready," she said.

He took the platter, on which another dinner was set out, and once again started up the staircase. How many times a day did he climb those stairs?

The difficulty was, while holding the platter with one hand and not spilling anything, to take the key from his

pocket and turn it in the lock, for that door was always kept locked, even when he was in the house. He turned the switch, and Kachoudas, across the street, saw the curtain light up. He set the platter down, always in the same place, and shut the door again behind him.

All this was very complicated. It had taken time to work it out. The hatter's comings and goings followed one another in a definite order which was immensely important.

First of all, he had to speak. He didn't always take the trouble to utter actual words, for downstairs it was at most heard only as a confused murmur. Today, for example, he repeated, not without satisfaction:

"You'd be making a mistake, Kachoudas!"

There was nothing especially good to eat that evening, but he picked out the tenderest piece of the veal cutlet. There were days when he ate the whole of the second dinner.

He went to the window. He had time. He moved the curtain aside a bit and spotted the little tailor, who, his dinner already eaten, was returning to his place on the table, while the little girls played on the floor in the front of the room and the eldest girl was undoubtedly washing the dishes with her mother.

As he went back to the tray he said aloud:

"Did you enjoy your dinner? Good!"

Then he went and emptied the dishes—except the bone from the cutlet—into the toilet bowl, but without pulling the chain to flush it. He'd done that in the beginning, but it was a mistake. There had been any number of mistakes and risky slips like that, which he'd corrected little by little.

He went downstairs again with the empty dishes, and Louise, the maid, finished eating her dinner in his place at the table. To save herself dishes to wash, she ate from her master's plate and drank from his glass. Like him, she read as she ate, choosing one or another of the

countless little books that are turned out for the nearly illiterate.

"Aren't you going out, Louise?"

"I don't want to get myself strangled."

"Good night."

"Good night, sir."

It was nearly done. A few more rites to get through— going to make sure that the shop door was properly shut, turning out the light, going up the stairs for the last time, taking his key from his pocket, opening the door, shutting it again.

Before long Louise would go upstairs to bed in the back room, and he would hear her heavy footsteps for fully a quarter of an hour before the mattress creaked under her weight.

"What a cow!"

He had a right to speak aloud. It was almost a necessity from time to time. Now he could flush the toilet in the bathroom, take off his necktie, his collar, his jacket, put on his brown dressing gown. Yet he was not entirely finished, for he still had to put three or four logs on the fire.

It was Louise who brought them up, every morning, and piled them on top of each other on the second-floor landing.

All the houses on that street were the same age, dated from Louis XIII. On the outside they had remained the same, with their arcades and their steeply pitched roofs, but with the passing centuries each of them had undergone various interior changes. For example, above Monsieur Labbé's head there was a third floor, but he could not get to it except by going out into the street. Beside the shop a door gave onto a narrow alley that led to the courtyard. And there was the foot of the stairway that gave access to the third floor, but without communicating with the second.

It had been practical, years ago, when there'd been

tenants upstairs. But the rooms had long been empty—precisely from the first year of Mathilde's illness, which had made the sound of footsteps overhead all day long intolerable to her.

It had taken a lawsuit to get rid of the people on the third floor. There'd been so many things more complicated than that!

Wasn't he forgetting something? The logs were blazing. The curtains were closed tight. He could put out the ceiling light—too glaring for his taste—and keep on only the lamp on the writing desk, for there'd always been a small desk in one corner, with a lot of little drawers, and now it was extremely useful.

He picked up the pile of newspapers, the scissors, filled his old meerschaum pipe. Once or twice he turned toward the window, thinking of Kachoudas.

"Poor wretch!"

At first putting together his letters had been a test of his patience, for he cut out each character separately. Now he was so familiar with the newspaper that he knew under which headline he was almost sure to find the words he needed. And in Mathilde's workbasket he had found a pair of embroidery scissors that cut without leaving any frayed edges.

The sixth woman is dead, young man, and again the whole city will mourn her fate.

He had got into the habit of addressing Jeantet directly.

Note that Mademoiselle Mollard has suffered from a heart condition for some years, that she lives alone, that she has no one to look after her, and that she has to give piano lessons to her friends' children. As to her brother-in-law, the architect, who makes a very good living, he has always refused to help her.

That is not why I killed her, of course. I killed her, like the others, because it had to be done. And that,

everyone refuses to believe. People will say again and write again that I am insane, a madman, a sadist, a monomaniac, and it is not true.

I do what I have to do, period.

If the public would only believe this, there would be an end to this stupid panic that keeps people from leaving their houses and has such a bad effect on business.

Unless someone sees fit to indulge in some foolish action, there is only one more name on my list. That will make exactly seven, and all the investigations in the world will not change it in the slightest.

In proof of which, young man, I now inform you that it will happen on Monday.

The address was easy to put together, for he had only to cut out Jeantet's signature at the end of an article and the address of the newspaper printed at the head of the Classified Advertising section.

Louise had just gone into her bedroom and was grunting as usual.

Monsieur Labbé sealed his letter, put a stamp on the envelope, and slipped it into the pocket of his jacket, which he had put on a coat hanger. Tomorrow morning, after taking the shutters down from his show window, he would wait for Valentin to arrive, then he would make his usual round of the city, whether it was raining or not.

The astonishing thing was that he hadn't had to change any of his habits. He'd always taken a morning walk around the nearest block or two of houses—just as, in the evening, he'd always gone to the Café des Colonnes.

It was half past nine. He still had a good hour before him, and he went and sat down in front of the fire, his legs stretched out, a thick book with yellowed pages open on his lap.

It was one of the volumes of the *Famous Trials of the 19th Century.*

He had bought twenty-odd volumes of it at the auction room a few months ago. He still had seven to read.

He was smoking in his usual way, taking little puffs at longish intervals. It was hot. Louise must have gone to sleep at last. All that he heard was the monotonous sound of the rain, sometimes a crackling from the logs, and there was no one to interrupt his reading.

Monsieur Labbé was calm, serene. From time to time he glanced at the alarm clock.

"Twenty minutes more!"

Ten more. Five more. At half past ten he shut his book with a sigh, stood up, and went into the bathroom. At a quarter before eleven he got into the right-hand bed.

Formerly there had been only one bed in the room, a very handsome bed that had gone well with the other pieces of furniture. When Mathilde had fallen ill, it had been carried—by way of the street, because there was no stairway between the second and third floors—to the empty apartment upstairs, and had been replaced by twin beds separated by a bedside table.

He turned his head to make sure that the still-smoldering logs in the fireplace were in no danger of rolling out onto the carpet and setting the room on fire.

Kachoudas, across the street, was still working. He was a poor lot. He did everything himself, including making trousers and waistcoats, which the better sort of tailors farm out to seamstresses who work at home.

Now that the room was dark Monsieur Labbé could see, through the curtain, the lighted rectangle on the other side of the street.

Before going to sleep he said, half aloud (for it was always a good idea to speak):

"Good night, Kachoudas."

He did not set the alarm: he woke of his own accord at half past five in the morning. That fat wench Louise was still asleep, snuggled down in her damp bed; she must

have heard him get up, go out on the landing for logs, shut the door again, light his fire. That morning, after a minute or two, he noticed that something was missing, and it was the spattering of the rain, the noise of water in the gutter pipe. It was still too dark to see the sky, but he could tell that a wind from the sea was driving the clouds inland.

He had to make his bed, tidy up the room, put the bucket with the ashes from the fire outside; he did all these things with precise movements, which he made in a carefully thought-out order.

He spoke a little, talking entirely at random, and soon saw the window across the street light up. It was not Kachoudas, who was still in bed, but his wife, who was lighting the fires in the house, sweeping the workroom, dusting.

He heard the carts passing on their way to the market, then there were others, which stopped in the street, voices of countrywomen, the thud of baskets and sacks being dropped on the pavement.

It was Saturday. He took his bath, dressed, while Louise washed herself just on the other side of the bathroom wall.

She went downstairs first to make the coffee, and when he went down himself the fire was lighted.

"Good morning, Louise."

"Good morning, sir."

In the hat shop he pushed a match into the little hole in the gas stove. The noises in the street were getting louder, but it wasn't yet time to take down the shutters.

First he had to eat his breakfast, then to take Mathilde's breakfast upstairs. The sky was beginning to grow pale. Monsieur Labbé rolled the armchair to the window, set it in the same place as always, made sure that the wooden head, which came from the workroom, wouldn't fall down.

Put out the light. Raise the blind. Everything was

gray, almost white. The rain had become a fog, and Kachoudas' lamp was visible only through a veil.

The windowpanes were frosted. Perhaps it would freeze at last? Bundled up in shawls, the countrywomen in the street stopped arranging their baskets now and again in order to beat their chilled blue hands against their thighs. One of them, a little old woman who had settled herself in the same spot for forty years, had lighted a brazier. At this time of year she sold chestnuts and walnuts.

Kachoudas had not yet got up onto his table. The kitchen door was open, and the whole family was eating breakfast. Madame Kachoudas had neither washed nor done up her hair. The youngest child, the only boy, who had big black almond-shaped eyes, was still in his nightgown.

They were an odd lot of people. They ate pork butcher's meat even at breakfast. Kachoudas had his back to the window, one shoulder higher than the other.

Monsieur Labbé would wait for him. There were still some little things he had to do. The newspapers from which he'd cut words and letters were already burned. He brought Louise the suit he'd worn the day before to be ironed, for he was very particular; his suits were always of broadcloth, his shoes made to order.

It had begun with the rumbling of a few carts, with a few scattered voices, and now, from one end of the street to the other, it had become the deafening uproar of every Saturday. He knew beforehand what odor of fresh vegetables, of wet cabbages, of poultry and rabbits, would assail his nostrils as soon as he opened his shop door.

He had still to wait a while, with his eye to the crack in the shutter, for Kachoudas finally to come out of his house; then he did likewise, calling over the heads of the market women:

"Good morning, Kachoudas."

The scrawny shoulders trembled, the man turned, opened his mouth, took several seconds before he brought out:

"Good morning, Monsieur Labbé."

For him, it must have been unbelievable, something verging on a hallucination. Was it perhaps the more so because of the fog? It was all happening just as on other mornings, or at least on other Saturdays; the hatter was freshly shaved, carefully dressed; in his dignified way he was taking down the shutters of his show window, taking them in one by one and putting them away in a space left for them behind the door.

The paved street was still wet, with puddles along the sidewalks. The pork butcher's shop next door to Kachoudas' house still had its lights on.

Valentin arrived at half past eight, looking flushed; he had scarcely got into the shop before he had to blow his nose.

"I've caught a cold," he said.

He'd be able to sweat it out in the already overheated air of the hat shop. Monsieur Labbé put on his overcoat, took down his hat.

"I'll be back in a quarter of an hour."

He made his way to the covered market, and many people greeted him, for he had been born in La Rochelle and had always lived there. He chose the mailbox in the Rue des Merciers; that morning there was no chance that anyone would notice him in the bustling crowd. Then, as he liked to do on a Saturday, he went into the covered market and looked over the displays in the fish and shellfish stands.

It was not until he was almost home that he bought the newspaper, at the corner of his own street; and he stuffed it into his pocket, not feeling curious enough even to glance at it.

A farmer's wife had brought in her son, and Valentin

was trying caps on him. It was the day for such customers. Monsieur Labbé went back and took off his overcoat and hat, then said to Louise through the partly open door:

"I want you to buy some crawfish. The little old woman from Charron has some fine ones. Has Madame called?"

"No, sir."

He would eat his portion of crawfish first, downstairs, and then Mathilde's in the bedroom. It was a piece of good luck that their former charwoman, Delphine, had gone to live with her daughter in the Île d'Oléron, for Delphine, who'd worked for them for twenty years, knew very well that Mathilde didn't like any kind of seafood.

He could have done better than to end up with Louise. Any number of things could have worked out more satisfactorily. He was even beginning to loathe the fat slut. She never asked a question. It was impossible to guess what she was thinking. Could it be that she never thought at all?

He didn't like her sleeping in the house. Delphine, who had children, had gone to her own place beyond the railroad station immediately after dinner. At first Louise had slept in the city too. Then, because of the murders of the old women, she had announced that she didn't want to go out after dark.

Why had he given in and arranged for her to have a room on the second floor? Was it that at the time he still had some vague idea in the back of his mind? When you didn't look at her too closely she was quite attractive. But now that he heard her making her toilet behind the bathroom wall, he couldn't help knowing that she wasn't very clean. The smell of her room, into which he'd happened to go, and her underwear thrown on a chair, had turned his stomach.

Probably she wasn't dangerous; even so, it was a complication, and he'd worked hard enough to avoid complications.

He'd see about it later on.

He changed his jacket—he always put on an old jacket to work in—then went back into the workroom and lighted the portable stove that he used for steaming his hats.

He opened a cupboard with the smallest key on his keyring. His keys, which were of crucial importance, were polished, shining like a set of tools, and he always kept them in the same pocket and never forgot to put them on the bedside table before he got into bed.

At the back of the closet a string hung from the ceiling, and he pulled it two or three times.

Valentin, still busy waiting on the woman with the little boy, took a few steps to inform him:

"Madame is calling you, Monsieur Labbé."

For by pulling the string he operated a mechanism that knocked on the floor upstairs, exactly as in the past, when, to summon him, Madame Labbé would knock on the same floor with her cane.

"I'll go up," he said, sighing.

Shut the closet door, pocket the keys again. Strangely enough, in Kachoudas' shop the little tailor was busy measuring a small boy whom his mother had brought in. A small boy and his mother on either side of the street—and, still stranger, from the same village.

He vanished up the spiral staircase, and Valentin could hear his footsteps. The door was shut again. The curtains made it impossible to see in from outside. In her kitchen Madame Kachoudas, who never gave a thought to her neighbors across the street, had her arms raised in the process of putting a dress over her underclothes; for the sake of warmth the Kachoudas tribe dressed, and even bathed, in the kitchen. For the little

girls and the little boy, they set an enamel basin on a chair.

He put another log on the fire, sat down, lighted his pipe, and only then opened the newspaper.

The Strangler has dispatched another victim.

Isn't it curious to observe how words can distort reality? *The Strangler!* With a capital into the bargain! As if, say, one was born a strangler! As if it was a vocation! When the truth was so different! It always irritated him a little. It was even a moment of irritation that had made him write his first letter to the newspaper. That time it had printed *A dangerous madman is loose in the city.*

He had replied:

No, sir, there is no madman. Do not talk about what you do not understand.

Yet that young Jeantet was not stupid. While the police were picking up vagabonds and sailors on a binge, questioning people in the streets and demanding their identity papers, the reporter was gradually building up a line of argument that made sense. After the third victim, Mademoiselle Lange, the old woman who kept the notions shop in the Rue Saint-Yon, and when police and voluntary measures were already in effect from nightfall on, he stated:

It is a mistake to spend time and effort on vagabonds and, in general, on all those who make themselves conspicuous by their clothing or their behavior. The murderer cannot but be a man who moves about unnoticed. Hence he is not a stranger to the city, as some have supposed. Given the comings and goings necessary for the commission of the three crimes, it is more than probable that he has at least once encountered one of the voluntary patrols that crisscross the city every evening.

He was right. The hatter had passed a patrol and had

calmly kept on his way. The beam of a flashlight had been thrown on him and held for a moment, while a voice said:

"Good evening, Monsieur Labbé."

"Good evening, gentlemen!"

. . . Only a well-known and respected citizen could have . . .

He went much further in his deductions—the young fellow who could be seen writing every evening at the first table in the Café des Colonnes:

. . . The times at which the attacks occur show that he is a married man with regular habits . . .

He based this statement on the fact that none of the crimes had been committed after the dinner hour.

. . . hence a man who does not go out alone in the evening . . .

From that point on, he went wrong. After the fifth murder, the one before the last, the murder of Léonide Proux, the midwife from Fétilly, he had written:

It is probable that the midwife was induced to go out by a telephone call, which seems to be confirmed by the case of instruments she was carrying when she was attacked. . . .

That was wrong. She was in fact the only one whom Monsieur Labbé had come upon almost by chance. She was on his list, sure enough. If he hadn't run into her, he might have telephoned to her, mightn't he?

. . . Since it would be dangerous to make such an incriminating call from a public telephone booth or a café . . .

He was trying to be too intelligent, more intelligent than the murderer. He even went so far as to insist that the latter had a telephone in his house. Didn't it occur to him that in that case his wife or the maid could have overheard the conversation?

And in fact Monsieur Labbé did not have a telephone, had always refused to have one in his house.

Young Jeantet went on floundering.

In all likelihood the perpetrator is a man who works in an office, which he leaves between five and six o'clock, and he commits his crimes before he gets home.

It was quite incomprehensible that he should write that at the café, where every day he saw businessmen and professional men spend an hour or two playing cards before dining.

Today there was something even better. The subhead of the story in the paper ran:

Have we a description of the murderer?

Mademoiselle Irène Mollard's body had been found shortly after 8:00 P.M. It had been a policeman who had literally stumbled over it. The whole street had been roused. The mother of the little girl to whom the old maid had given her last music lesson had testified in great excitement:

"I felt very strongly that I oughtn't to let her go alone. I begged her to wait for my husband to get home; he would have seen her all the way to her door. She wouldn't hear of it. She laughed at my fears. She insisted that she didn't feel afraid. When she started off, I kept the door part way open for a while so I could hear her footsteps. And now I remember that I saw a man in the middle of the street. I nearly called for help, then I thought it would be silly, that a murderer wouldn't just stand there right in the middle of the street. Even so, I shut the door very fast. I didn't see him well at all, but I'm almost certain he was short and slight and had on a raincoat that was too long for him."

Kachoudas' raincoat—or, rather, the raincoat that didn't belong to Kachoudas but that a traveling salesman visiting the city had left at his house because it was worn and soiled one day when he'd bought an overcoat from him, and which the little tailor wore for reasons of economy when it rained.

Monsieur Labbé turned to face the window. Ka-

choudas had got up on his table again. He was speaking to his wife, who was ready to go out, with a shopping bag in her hand. Was she asking him what he would like to eat? Probably.

The tailor hadn't yet read the newspaper. He went out of his house in the morning only to take down the shutters. Later, when she came back from the market, his wife would bring him the *Écho des Charentes*.

Louise was going out to market too. The bell on the front door had just tinkled several times. There were customers in the shop.

Before leaving the bedroom, Monsieur Labbé didn't forget to mutter a few words, and he changed the position of the armchair a little.

Valentin saw his legs, his body, and then his calm, untroubled face appear. Since he seemed embarrassed, the hatter asked him:

"What's the matter?"

And the snuffling young man pointed to a huge peasant swaying from one foot to the other.

"The gentleman needs an eight and a half and we have only an eight."

"Let me see."

He reshaped the hat with steam, and the customer left, looking at himself in the mirrors a little uncomfortably.

3

"You'll shut up the shop, Valentin."

"Yes, sir. Good night, sir."

"Good night, Valentin."

Valentin had been blowing his nose all day, and it was so runny that it made your eyes water to see and hear him. Twice he had taken advantage of a time when there were no customers and had hung his handkerchief in front of the gas radiator to dry.

He was a poor wretch too. He was tall and red-haired, with china-blue eyes and an expression so guileless that Monsieur Labbé, opening his mouth to say something to him, would often shut it again without speaking and merely shrug his shoulders. They spent the greater part of the day together, for actually there was no division between the hat shop and the workroom. On some days hours would go by without a customer appearing. When he'd dusted everything, put everything in order, checked the price tags and labels for the hundredth time, poor Valentin, like a big dog embarrassed by the size of his body, would look for some corner in which to keep out of the way, taking care not to make a noise, giving a start at his employer's least movement, and, since he was not allowed to smoke in the shop, quietly sucking violet-flavored candies.

"See you on Monday, Valentin. Have a pleasant Sunday."

It was a sort of extra pat, given in passing.

What mattered was to find out whether Kachoudas would come downstairs or not. He hadn't stirred out of his house all day. Once, he'd come down for a fitting,

another time he'd unrolled suitings for a customer who hadn't made up his mind and had had to get out of it by promising to come back. He'd kept a light on in his workroom, for the fog hadn't lifted, and when the noises from the market had lessened, the sound of the whistling buoy could be heard at regular intervals. It filled all space like the bellowing of some monstrous cow, and there were people who had long lived in the city and were still moved by it. Not a boat had gone out. Some that were expected had not come in, and there was fear for their safety.

The peasant women had gone off in their carts or by bus well before nightfall, and only the men were left lingering in the bars, their faces flushed, their eyes bright.

Kachoudas had read the newspaper. At any rate, his wife had brought it to him. Monsieur Labbé had made no mistake about that. Did he ever make a mistake? That was something he couldn't allow himself. In spite of carrying so much in his mind, he managed not to forget anything, not the least detail. Otherwise, indeed, he'd be a lost man.

The newspaper was on a chair near the tailor's table, and it had obviously been opened.

Kachoudas would come. The hatter was convinced that he'd come, and he stood in his doorway, looked up at the lighted window, and repeated mechanically, like a farmer's wife calling hens:

"Here, chick, chick, chick, chick . . ."

He walked noiselessly, and he had scarcely gone twenty yards when, there behind him, he heard the footsteps he could tell from all others.

Kachoudas had come. Had he hesitated? A poor wretch—no doubt of it. There were lots of them in this world. He must be terribly eager to get his hands on the twenty thousand francs. He'd never even seen such an

amount of money all at once, unless perhaps behind the grille in a bank. It took him two years, working day and night on his table, to earn as much as that.

He certainly wanted to earn those twenty thousand francs. He wanted it with all his strength. It was even because he wanted it so desperately that he was so afraid.

Was he perhaps even more afraid of losing them than afraid of the hatter? What had happened was what had been bound to happen: it's always a fellow like Kachoudas who gets himself suspected; it was Kachoudas whom the mother of the little girl at the piano had seen and described to the police.

They walked on, one behind the other, as they did every day, and at every step the little tailor couldn't help throwing one leg out to the side. Monsieur Labbé, on the contrary, walked calmly and with dignity; he really had a fine gait.

He pushed open the door of the Café des Colonnes, and the noise and the smell alone would have told him that it was a Saturday. Yes, the smell—for the people who came on Saturdays didn't order the same drinks as the customers on other days.

The room was crammed. Some people were even standing. The ordinary peasants went to the little bars near the market; here, it was the richer and the more enterprising sort, the ones who had business to do with the fertilizer dealers, the insurance agents, the lawyers who set up shop every Saturday at tables that, for a few hours, became their desks or their counters.

Only the tables in the middle, near the stove, remained an oasis that was respected, surrounded by a zone of calm and silence.

Chantreau, the doctor, who was not playing, was seated behind the senator, who was holding cards. Monsieur Labbé touched his hand:

"Good evening, Paul."

And, as his friend took a pill from a small cardboard box:

"Something wrong?"

"My liver."

It came over him periodically. From one day to the next he would look thinner by several pounds: his face was ravaged, with soft bags under the eyes, the expression that of a man who suffers.

They were the same age. At school the two of them had been great friends, almost inseparable.

Gabriel took Monsieur Labbé's coat and hat.

"The usual?"

In front of the doctor, on the marble table, there was a half bottle of Vichy water. Kachoudas, who had just come in, hesitated to sit near the cardplayers.

He was a poor wretch too! Not only Kachoudas, who'd just lowered the tips of his buttocks onto a chair, but also Paul, the doctor. Monsieur Labbé must still have, buried in some drawer, a photograph showing them both at fifteen or sixteen. At that age Chantreau was thin, his hair with a touch of red, but not the same sandstone red as Valentin's; he held his chin up proudly, looked challengingly in front of him.

He had already made up his mind to be a doctor. But not an ordinary doctor—he'd be a great discoverer like Pasteur and Nicolle. His father was rich, owned a dozen farms in the Aunis and the Vendée. His only occupation was to manage them from a distance, and, oddly enough, he spent every afternoon at the Café des Colonnes, at the same table that the bridge players occupied nowadays.

"He makes me sick," young Paul said of him. "He's a miser. He doesn't give a damn about the condition of the peasants."

In general, the parents of all of them were well off,

owned estates of farms or houses, or else boats or shares in boats.

Kachoudas kept looking hard at him on the sly, and Monsieur Labbé pretended not to notice it. It was a game. It proved to him that his mind was unperturbed. The roles were reversed: it was the little tailor who was sweating with fear, drinking nervously, at times even seemed to be begging him for something.

For what? To let himself be caught, so the fellow could pocket the twenty-thousand-franc reward?

"You're drinking too much, Paul."

"I know."

"Why?"

He had come back to the city and opened an office. He had decided:

"I will see patients only in the morning, then I'll be free the rest of the time to do my research."

He had treated himself to a real laboratory and subscribed to all the medical journals.

"Why have you never married, Paul?"

Perhaps because he'd wanted to become a great scientist; he didn't know for sure, and he let it go at shrugging his shoulders, with a grimace wrung from him by pain.

He had let his beard grow and given up on his general appearance. His fingernails were black, his linen dubious. At first he had come to the Café des Colonnes at six o'clock, like a man who worked, then at five, then at four, and now he got there right after lunch; since nobody was there at that hour to make up a foursome, he played checkers with Oscar, the proprietor.

He had finally turned sixty, like Monsieur Labbé. They had all turned sixty.

"Will you sit in for me, Léon? I have to go and talk to my constituents."

André Laude, the senator, who had just won a rubber, rose reluctantly. Around them there was a continuous

commotion—shoe soles scuffing through the sawdust on the floor, glasses clinking, saucers, voices louder than usual.

"They'll catch him in the end, I agree," said a farmer wearing leather gaiters. "They all end by letting themselves get caught, even the smartest of them. And after that? You'll see—they'll ship him off to an asylum on the grounds that he's crazy, and we taxpayers will support him till he dies."

"Unless he happens on a young fellow like me!"

"You? You'll do just like the others, for all your big mouth. You may hit him in the jaw once with that fist of yours, but then you'll obediently hand him over to the police. I won't say it mightn't be different in a village. A man can lay his hands on a pitchfork or a shovel there."

Without turning a hair, Monsieur Labbé sat calmly down in the chair left vacant by the senator, who was beginning to make his round of the tables. For a moment the hatter wondered if Kachoudas had caught a cold too, his face was so red and his eyes so bright, but then he noticed two saucers under his glass.

The tailor was drinking! Could it be to give himself courage? Even now he was signaling Gabriel to serve him a third glass of white wine.

"We're partners," declared Julien Lambert, the insurance agent, shuffling the cards.

He didn't drink—that is, he stopped at an apéritif, or at the most two. He was a Protestant. He had four or five children, and he would have had more if his wife hadn't had a miscarriage every other time. It was a subject for jokes. People would ask him:

"Your wife?"

"In the hospital."

"Baby?"

"Miscarriage."

He too had money, which he'd inherited from his

parents; it had enabled him to buy an insurance business. He didn't devote much time to it. He had good salesmen. Sometimes one of them would come to the café for him about some urgent piece of business. After playing bridge in the afternoon, he dined in a hurry in order to play bridge again either at home or at some friend's house.

As it happened he was the brother of Madame Geoffroy-Lambert, who had lived in the Rue Réaumur, the fourth old woman to have been strangled. Monsieur Labbé had gone to her funeral.

"My heartfelt sympathy, Julien."

He had gone to all the funerals, for he knew them all, at least through Mathilde.

The young journalist was not to be seen. No doubt he was busy somewhere else with his investigation. Two or three times Monsieur Labbé looked in the direction of his usual table.

"We've received another letter," said Caillé, the printer and owner of the *Écho des Charentes.*

"He's beginning to go a bit far," muttered Julien Lambert, at the same time bidding two clubs.

Then, turning to Chantreau, who was watching the course of the game:

"Do you think he's insane, Paul?"

The doctor shrugged his shoulders. It didn't interest him at the moment. All he cared about was the clawing pain in his abdomen.

"In any case, he won't stop till he's caught," he growled.

"Jack the Ripper was never caught, and he stopped killing."

This pleased Monsieur Labbé, who hadn't thought of it.

"How many did he kill?" he asked. "Three diamonds."

"Pass."

"Three spades," Lambert raised him.

"Four hearts."

He had a little slam in prospect, and there was a moment of silence, broken by successive bids, which went up to six diamonds.

"Doubled!"

"I don't know how many he killed, but the terror all over London and the suburbs lasted for several months. The army was called out. Offices and factories had to shut down because the clerks and workers wouldn't risk going out in the streets."

"I'd be curious to know how many women there are in the streets at this moment."

The little tailor was trembling, and he emptied his third glass at one gulp. No longer daring to look toward the cardplayers for fear of meeting the hatter's eyes, he stared dismally at the dirty floor.

"Four trumps. I finesse the king of spades and the remaining tricks are good in my hand."

It would be interesting to know what Kachoudas was like when he'd been drinking. Monsieur Labbé had never seen him drunk. The doctor, for example, who began soaking it up in the morning after each patient and who didn't stop all day long, first got into a mood of slightly ironic benevolence. He would address his last patients every morning as:

"My child."

Or:

"Old chap."

Or:

"My dear lady."

And instead of writing prescriptions for them he would go to his cupboard for some medicine or other and insist on their taking it free of charge.

By the beginning of the afternoon he displayed an Olympian majesty, his face wreathed in a nimbus of

smoke, his gestures deliberate, his eyes heavy, his words few and far between. Then, little by little, he became sarcastic, even with his best friends.

People who ran into him about ten o'clock in the evening, when he was on his way home after drinking red wine in various little bars, claimed that by then he was tearful and took them by the arm.

"A failure, old man, a stinking old failure—that's what I am! Admit you're disgusted with me, all of you!"

As for Oscar, the proprietor, whose profession obliged him to drink little nips all day with his customers, his eyes became swollen, his manner both dignified and uncertain, his speech thick, and, by evening, he slurred his syllables so that it wasn't always possible to understand what he was saying.

In any case, the little tailor was becoming feverish. He couldn't sit still, made unexpected movements like tics or as if he were chasing away a swarm of flies.

Monsieur Labbé had the agreeable feeling that he had him on the end of a string, was sweetly murmuring to him:

"Take it easy, little fellow!"

He knew perfectly well that Inspector Pigeac was there, directly behind him at the table where the men from forty to fifty sat. He had seen him come in wearing a gray overcoat, with a gray hat on his head, and his face gray. He reminded him of a fish, of a lusterless cod; there was always a cold smile on his lips, as if in token that he knew what was what.

He knew absolutely nothing. Monsieur Labbé was convinced of that. He was a pompous idiot, a born bureaucrat who thought about nothing but getting promoted and had joined a Masonic lodge because he'd been led to believe it would give him a boost. He was good at nothing but billiards, at which he managed to

make runs of a hundred and fifty and two hundred, circling slowly around the green-covered table and occasionally looking at himself in the mirrors.

"Don't go there, little fellow."

It was to Kachoudas he said it, under his breath, for he sensed the state the little tailor was in: his head was beginning to whirl, he felt hot, he didn't know which way to look, he was thinking of his twenty thousand francs and of what the mother of the little girl at the piano had testified.

"He claims," Caillé, the printer, went on, "that he'll kill only one more."

"Why?"

"He doesn't give any reason. He keeps insisting that it's a necessity, that he doesn't do it on impulse. You can read his letter in the paper tomorrow. My bid? One no trump."

Four glasses of white wine. Kachoudas had already drunk four glasses of white wine; it was making him forget to look at the clock. The time when he usually went home had gone by.

"It's to be on Monday."

"What is?"

"The last murder. Why Monday, I have no idea. I'll be delighted to see if there are any murders today or tomorrow. That would show that he writes whatever comes into his head."

"He certainly doesn't do that," Julien Lambert declared.

"And why my sister, who's never harmed a living soul?"

"Maybe he doesn't like old women," Chantreau said thickly.

Monsieur Labbé looked at him curiously, for his idea wasn't all that stupid. It wasn't exactly right, but it certainly wasn't stupid.

"Have you noticed," Caillé went on, "that they're all more or less our age?"

Then Arnould, "Fatty" Arnould, the Arnould of the sardine fleet, who so far had said nothing, put in his oar:

"There are two of them I've slept with, and one that I nearly married."

Lambert took offense.

"My sister?"

"I don't mean your sister."

But everyone knew that Madame Geoffroy-Lambert had been liberal about opening her thighs. It was true that that sort of thing hadn't begun for her until she was nearly forty and had been widowed, and that she only took on very young men.

"Did you know Irène Mollard?"

"She was pretty, but so frail even at seventeen that everyone thought she was ripe for the grave. Sentimental as a popular novel. So sentimental that she never married. I bet she died a virgin."

"Is that so?" someone asked the doctor, whose patient she had been.

"I had no occasion to examine her gynecologically."

"Who bid three clubs? We were at three clubs. Your bid, Paul."

The café was full of smoke, which was attracted toward the big spherical light shades; they were a milky white and had been put up only recently. The senator had reached his third table, and at each one he stood a round of drinks. At nearly every table he would take out a notebook and jot down a word or two. The voters who didn't ask him for something were much in the minority, and when Monsieur Labbé looked across at him just as he was putting his notebook back in his pocket, Laude gave him a cynical wink.

He'd been the poorest of them, in the old days. His father was a minor employee in the Crédit Lyonnais.

The son had married an only daughter when he was still no more than a lawyer and a town councilor. Today he lived in one of the big mansions in the Rue Réaumur, not far from Madame Geoffroy-Lambert's.

"Come to think of it," said Monsieur Labbé, "your sister's house must be up for sale."

"Are you planning to buy it?" asked Lambert ironically. "It's a white elephant, that house. It has only eleven bedrooms and stabling for ten horses at the back of the courtyard. I'm trying to interest the Prefecture; they're always in need of office space."

"Take it easy, little fellow!"

Monsieur Labbé was almost ready to order Gabriel not to serve the little tailor anything more to drink, and Gabriel would certainly have obeyed him. He had an anxious moment when Kachoudas jumped up as if propelled by a spring and seemed about to rush over to the inspector's table. But he went on beyond it and plunged into the washroom.

His bladder? His bowels? As luck would have it, Monsieur Labbé was dummy just then, so he followed Kachoudas into the washroom—purely out of curiosity, for he wasn't afraid.

It was only his bladder, and there they were standing side by side in front of the white porcelain that covered the wall.

The little tailor, who was shaking in every limb, couldn't run away. After hesitating a moment, Monsieur Labbé said quietly, looking straight ahead:

"Take it easy, Kachoudas."

They were alone together. Did the tailor suppose his neighbor was going to strangle him? Monsieur Labbé could have assured him—and truthfully—that he didn't have his instrument with him.

As a matter of fact, no one had thought of making a list of the inhabitants of La Rochelle who played the cello. There couldn't be so very many of them.

As for him, people had probably forgotten he was a musician. It was at least twenty years since he'd played his cello, and the instrument was in the attic. To get to the attic, you had to go out of the house, enter the blind alley, and climb the stairs to the third floor. This was what he'd done, for he wasn't careless enough to buy a cello string at the violin maker's shop in the Rue du Palais. More especially since there was only one such shop in the city. And it had been fifteen years since the hatter had left La Rochelle, even to go to Rochefort— fifteen years during which he had not once slept anywhere but in his own bed.

No one had thought of that, either. The others occasionally failed to appear for the regular afternoon meeting. André Laude went to Paris for the Senate sittings and spent his vacations in a château in the Dordogne which his wife had brought him as part of her dowry. Chantreau himself took the waters at Vichy once a year.

Julien Lambert's family owned a small house at Fourras, where they all spent two months a year, and sometimes the insurance agent would announce that he was going to Bordeaux on business, sometimes that he was off for Paris.

Most of them had automobiles or took trains. Arnould, the shipowner, had taken a cruise to Spitsbergen the previous summer. There were days when it was hard to find a fourth for bridge, and once in a while men from the forty-to-fifty-year table had had to be called to the rescue.

It was only the hatter who was always there, and people had got so accustomed to it that no one thought there was anything odd about it. How long had it been since he'd seen a real cow—not counting the herds that went through the streets on their way to the slaughterhouse?

At first people had felt sorry for him. They had felt even sorrier for Mathilde.

"How does she put up with it?"

"Pretty well, pretty well."

Kachoudas himself . . . Kachoudas had been to Paris

and Elbeuf! On certain summer Sundays Kachoudas would take his family to the seashore—not very far, it was true, just to Châtelaillon—and on those days the street was as empty as a billiard table, without a sound except the sparrows chirping.

Monsieur Labbé had been the first to return to his place. He knew very well that the other would follow.

"The three hearts?"

"I made five."

"You muffed that hand. Is it my deal?"

It was six o'clock, and the peasants were thinning out. The ones who still stayed on were those who owned a car or a pickup truck, for the carts, which had left long ago, were being driven along the country roads at a walk in the fog that was thickening again. It was so dense, even in the city, that when the café door opened it poured into the room like cold smoke, whiter than the smoke from the pipes and cigars.

Who, except the men at their table, would have believed that Monsieur Labbé had been an aviator? Yet he had been, during World War I. He had shot down enemy planes like clay pipes in a shooting gallery, he had earned several citations. He had even founded an aviation club at La Rochelle, had been its president for some time. And before that he had done his military service in the dragoons.

"I double the two clubs."

"I redouble."

He never made a mistake. Julien Lambert, who was always finicky, had not had a single criticism to make of him. His bids were correct, his finesses almost always well planned.

Wouldn't the simplest thing be to give Kachoudas the twenty thousand francs? He could indulge himself that

far. He was well off. If he was letting his hat shop go to pot, it was because he wanted to.

He could have moved, since business was shifting to the Rue du Palais, where the lights and the phonographs of Prisunic and the other big shops shattered the air.

Even in the Rue du Minage it would be easy to light his show window more brightly, modernize the shop, repaint the walls and the shelves in light colors.

What was the use? His friends seldom bought a hat from him; they preferred to get their hats in Bordeaux or Paris. He was satisfied with reblocking them in his workroom, opening the closet occasionally to pull the string.

"Madame Labbé is calling you," Valentin would say at once, as if he'd been the only one to hear the knocking on the ceiling.

He frowned when he heard Kachoudas say to Gabriel, hesitantly:

"A brandy!"

So he'd decided to get drunk, and he looked away to avoid meeting the hatter's eyes.

Would he, quite soon now, have the courage to climb up on his table, pick up a piece of cloth that smelled of wool grease? After all, the fellow had his table, the bulb hooked onto a wire, the bit of chalk on its string. He had his smell too, which he took with him everywhere and which was only unpleasant to outsiders, which he must himself inhale with a sort of sensual pleasure. And his wife, always slatternly, with the sharp voice that he heard all day through the partly open kitchen door, the little girls, the boy, achieved at last after four girls, the eldest of whom must be beginning to have sweethearts.

One of these days Madame Kachoudas would be pregnant again. It was amazing that she'd gone for three years without. Unless there was something wrong with her insides?

When they left the café, Monsieur Labbé could speak

to the tailor in the street, calm him, reassure him, ask him to wait for a minute, and go and get him twenty thousand francs. There was a bulging wallet in the desk in the bedroom that held more than that in banknotes. It went back to the days of Mathilde, who distrusted everything and everybody and had no faith in banks.

"Gabriel!"

"Yes, Monsieur Labbé. The same?"

"A brandy-and-water."

Kachoudas' brandy had made him want to drink one too, but he wouldn't get drunk; he had seldom got drunk in his life, except when he was a student and during the war, before he started out on a raid.

"I ruff."

Chantreau, sitting beside him, swallowed another pill, and Monsieur Labbé received his bad breath straight in the face.

"Your wife?"

"Still the same."

"She doesn't get bedsores?"

He shook his head.

"She's lucky."

It had been some ten years since a doctor had entered the house. At the beginning of her paralysis, Mathilde had wanted to see them all. There was a new one every week. He called in specialists from Bordeaux, from Paris. She had undergone every possible kind of medical treatment: then it had been the turn of the priests, the nuns, and for two years in succession she had made the journey to Lourdes.

Altogether, this state of agitation had lasted for five years, with ups and downs, crises of mysticism, periods of hope and periods of resignation.

"Swear to me that if I 'pass away,' you won't marry again."

The next day she would take his hand, look at him protectively:

"Listen, Léon. When I am gone, you mustn't go on by yourself. You'll find some fine girl to marry, and perhaps she'll give you children. You must give her my jewels. Yes! I insist."

For a week she would read from dawn to dark, and the next week she would spend her time staring angrily at the curtains.

She had sent to Charron for the healer, in whom she'd believed for nearly a month. She had got tired of five nurses, and the last one had been treated to a stream of insults.

One fine day she had decided that she'd have no more doctors and no more priests, and a little later she had told Delphine, who was their charwoman at the time, that she was never to cross the threshold of her room again.

Chantreau, who had no wife, spent his solitary days drinking. Julien Lambert had a wife—a big brunette—and children, and he killed time playing cards.

As for Arnould, of the sardine fleet, who had divorced his first wife and married a woman fifteen years younger than himself, he went to a brothel at least twice a week; he'd even fallen asleep there after drinking too much.

It was Caillé who stopped the inspector as he brushed past their table.

"How's your investigation going, Pigeac?"

"Well enough, well enough," he answered enigmatically.

(Idiot! Pompous idiot!)

"Did you get the copy of the letter we received by the afternoon mail?"

"I've read it."

"What do you think of it?"

"That he'll very soon get himself caught."

"Have you a clue?"

Monsieur Labbé looked at Kachoudas, whose nervous tension was painful to see.

"If he tries anything on Monday it'll be his last move. But he's bluffing, I assure you."

"Jeantet claims he isn't."

"Of course if that's Monsieur Jeantet's opinion—" said Pigeac sarcastically.

"He insists that the man isn't lying."

"Really?"

"This 'necessity' he talks about is disturbing. You understand what I mean? As Jeantet wrote—and very rightly—he doesn't give the impression that he picks his victims at random."

"My congratulatons to your reporter."

And the inspector bit off the end of a cigar and gave an exaggerated smile.

"Why seven, and why Monday?"

"I have to leave you, gentlemen. Excuse me."

When the inspector had gone, Caillé muttered:

"He's annoyed. I know perfectly well that Jeantet is only a boy. I took him on practically out of charity, because his mother, who's a widow, has to go out as a charwoman. But I'll bet that if the murderer is ever discovered, it'll be Jeantet who'll discover him."

"Let's talk about something else," Julien Lambert proposed. "It's your deal."

It was half past six, and Monsieur Labbé asked:

"Is the rubber finished? If you don't mind, I'll let someone else take my place."

They never insisted with him—as they did with the others—because of Mathilde. He received special consideration. Everyone had a particular way of saying how-do-you-do to him, of shaking his hand. It had become a habit. When he was gone, there was always someone to murmur:

"Poor chap!"

But the tone was always forced. As it has been when people condoled with Julien Lambert after his sister had been strangled.

One of them—it had been the doctor, one evening when he had been drinking heavily—had even gone so far as to growl:

"Out of them all, she was probably the only one who felt sorry she hadn't been raped!"

"See you tomorrow, gentlemen."

"You're forgetting that tomorrow is Sunday."

It was true. They didn't meet on Sundays.

"Till Monday, then."

The day for the last victim! After that, it would be over. People would talk about it for a while longer, then they'd begin thinking of other things and no one would mention the old women, who would gradually pass into legend.

It was almost a pity. He looked at the little tailor, and he, as if obeying him, made his way to the rack on which he had hung his overcoat. It was not the raincoat he had worn the day before. He hadn't dared to wear it. He would never wear it again. Who knew if he hadn't destroyed it?

Monsieur Labbé walked calmly across the café, and his eyes met Mademoiselle Berthe's. She was sitting near the window, in the place that Jeantet had occupied the evening before. She came to the Colonnes fairly often, two or three times a week. You smelled her perfume right away. She dressed prettily, always in black and white, which suggested mourning and made her more exciting.

She was drinking her glass of port in her ladylike way, sitting alone. She would give a discreet smile, barely perceptible, when one of the men whom she knew looked at her, but she never spoke to any of them.

Monsieur Labbé would only have had to wink and walk slowly to the Rue Gargoulleau, where she had a charming apartment.

It would have been a good trick to play on Kachoudas. What would the tailor have thought? That he was going

to strangle Mademoiselle Berthe, though she was scarcely thirty-five years old?

Louise, his maid, would be waiting for him. He invariably sat down to dinner at seven o'clock. He would leave it for next week, when everything would be finished and it would serve as a pleasant little reward.

Come along, Kachoudas! Follow me, my good man! No old woman today, and no young one, either. We're going home.

The little tailor's footsteps, behind him, sounded uncertain. He must have been thinking of speaking to the hatter, for at one moment, as they were going along the Rue du Minage, his step became quicker, more hurried. He got within a few yards of Monsieur Labbé, in the fog that turned him into a phantom bigger than life.

All things considered, they were both afraid. Monsieur Labbé involuntarily walked faster. He had just thought:

"Suppose he's armed? Suppose he's going to shoot me?"

Kachoudas was overexcited enough for that.

But no. He stopped, let the distance between them increase, started off again, groping along through the dark. Each of them finally came to a stop in front of his house, took his key from his pocket, and in the silence of the street Monsieur Labbé's calm voice came through the fog:

"Good night, Kachoudas."

He waited, with his key in the lock, his heart skipping a beat. A few seconds passed, and an uncertain voice stammered out reluctantly:

"Good night, Monsieur Labbé."

4

He saw light under the door, heard soft footsteps on the stairs, which meant that it was Sunday. On that day he got up a little later than on weekdays; the maid, on the other hand, would manage to drag herself out of bed even before the whistle of the earliest train had sounded. Blear-eyed, she would go downstairs to the kitchen, light the fire, and stand there dozing while great pans of water were getting hot.

The first Sunday she had been in the house, he had gone downstairs out of curiosity. He had found the glazed half of the kitchen door curtained by a towel held in place by thumbtacks.

"What is it?" Louise had asked crossly.

"It's me."

"Do you want something? You can see for yourself I'm washing."

Probably in the tub that was used for the laundry. It must have been the way things were done at her home in Charron, and at Kachoudas' house. And all that day the kitchen smelled of bath soap.

Monsieur Labbé couldn't let her use his bathroom, for she would have to go through the bedroom to get to it. He had bought her a zinc tub. So now on Sunday he heard her filling it with jugs of hot water, which she carried upstairs one by one, panting. If on other mornings she sometimes didn't even bother to wash her face, on Sundays she would spend an hour sitting in her tub, washing every cranny.

This rather disgusted the hatter. He had never liked the smell of other people, never liked being close to anyone. Yet he had lived for fifteen years in this bed-

room with a powerless woman who could do nothing for herself and who became furious when anyone made a move to open the window.

Perhaps it wasn't her fault; hadn't he better just blame it on the state of her health? During the last years, in any case, Mathilde was so dirty that it sometimes seemed as if she was doing it on purpose, to defy him. She'd even go so far as to ask him:

"You think I smell bad, don't you?"

He went and crouched down in front of the fireplace to light the logs. He never made a botch of lighting his fire; it would be only a few minutes before it was burning brightly. It was colder than it had been on the previous days, with a different kind of cold. Moving the curtain aside a little, he saw the night sky very clear, icy, and touching the windowpane chilled his fingertips.

So the rain was over. The whole city would be glad. Not he. It had come one day too early. It was as if the sky had betrayed him, a sort of personal defeat. He'd have liked to finish it off in the same sort of atmosphere. It wasn't only that the rain in the dark streets, with a halo around every light and reflections on the pavement, had aroused a certain excitement in him; it had also made his movements easier. There were fewer people in the streets. And what people there were walked close to the houses, thinking only of protecting themselves from the rain and the mud in the streets.

In Kachoudas' house no one was up yet. Not a light. The little tailor was asleep, lying against his fat, kind-hearted wife; after the drinking he'd done the evening before, he must have been restless all night; had he snored, even talked aloud?

She had not reproached him when he'd got home. Yet he had hardly entered the warm house when his drunkenness had become more marked, probably because of the change from the cold outside. He had

started up the spiral staircase (the same as the one at Monsieur Labbé's), forgetting to shut up the shop and put out the lights, which he always did himself; and as soon as he got to the workroom he had dropped into a chair, with one arm on the back of it and his face on his bent arm.

Was he crying? It was not unlikely. Or did he feel ill? His son, who was three and a half or four years old, had come and circled curiously around him; so did the two little girls, and finally Madame Kachoudas had come out of her kitchen carrying a hot iron. She had immediately realized what was up and had said nothing, her lips hadn't even moved; she had vanished into the other room, from which, a few minutes later, she had reappeared with a bowl of black coffee.

"Drink it, Kachoudas."

She called him Kachoudas. Nobody called the tailor by his Christian name. Even on the signboard there was only his family name, which was more than likely a clan name that must be common in hundreds of villages in the Near East.

Kachoudas had finally uncovered his face, and it was clear, even from across the street, that he felt ashamed. He asked his wife some question—was it whether the children had seen him in that state? She had helped him drink his coffee, and after swallowing scarcely half of it he'd had to run for the far end of the room.

Monsieur Labbé had not seen him all evening. It was Madame Kachoudas who had come downstairs to put up the blinds and padlock the door. She had put out the light in the workroom and had gone on working in the kitchen when everyone else was in bed.

It was Sunday, and the sun would almost certainly be out. Monsieur Labbé went through the usual routine, made his bed with clean sheets, took the week's soiled sheets and towels out onto the landing, ran water into

the bathtub, and didn't forget to speak from time to time, saying anything, it didn't matter what, to keep up the illusion.

In the course of the years he had come to regulate his movements in a sort of ballet. It had become automatic; he no longer needed to think. This was so much the case that when, for some unexpected reason, the rhythm changed, he would be left unable to move for a moment, completely at a loss, like a broken-down machine, before he could get going again. For example, while the bathtub was filling he had time to put his clothes into the wardrobe, the coat on a hanger, the trousers neatly creased, then to lay out his socks, shirt, collar, and necktie on the foot of the bed. There was a time for everything, and he very seldom altered the order of his acts.

If you took the trouble to count, there were hundreds of them, possibly thousands, which, put end to end, finished by filling up the day, and he performed them with a certain satisfaction, especially on Sunday, for he knew that after the early-morning ritual he would enjoy a long free day, all alone in the house.

When he went downstairs, he had already got ahead of his schedule: he had pushed Mathilde's armchair in front of the window, with the wooden head at the right angle, and raised the blind though it wasn't yet daylight.

He found Louise by the kitchen stove, holding a bowl of coffee with milk, fully dressed and ready to go out, in her Sunday dress and coat and with her hat on.

"Everything you'll need is in the pantry," she announced in her flat voice, which was like a denial of the joy of life.

She was stupid, dumb as one of the beasts on her father's farm. Better not to pay any attention to it. Every Sunday she took the early bus to Charron, where she spent the day with her family and her girl friends.

She had a way of looking at Monsieur Labbé that he

had never managed to get used to. She would stare at him as if she didn't see him. Or else she saw him differently from other people, and sometimes that made him uneasy. What did she think of him? Mustn't she think it was a pretty odd household? Did she hide her thoughts? Did she think at all?

"Is Madame all right?"

"The same as usual. Thank you, Louise."

He preferred waiting for her to leave before he sat down to breakfast, for her presence was enough to spoil his pleasure. He went and closed the shop door after her, listened to her footsteps receding along the sidewalk, louder than elsewhere because of the arcades, and the church bells began to ring.

He had always had a particular liking for Sunday, even in Mathilde's time, when it had kept him tied upstairs and brought only hours of intense boredom. Could it be that he had grown used to boredom, had come to like it?

He read as he ate. He was reading an analysis of the trial of an agitator who, in 1882 in the Jura, had roused the mob to such enthusiasm that a revolution had almost broken out and the army had had to be sent for. It didn't much matter what he read. He would have forgotten it the next day. He bought his books at the auction room, two houses beyond his own, picking them out at random, one day novels, another day historical studies. They were invariably books with yellowed pages, which gave off a special smell and in which he would sometimes find a pressed flower, sometimes a squashed fly. Once in a while he would even find a letter in faded ink that had served as a bookmark, and it was seldom that there wasn't a name written on the flyleaf or the purple stamp of some public library.

Today he had promised himself that he would get through an important piece of work. He'd been wanting to do it for a long time. But first he got up and went and washed his cup and plate under the faucet, then shook

out the tablecloth and swept up the floor where there were some scattered bread crumbs. He also went to the pantry to see what Louise had got ready for his lunch, and he was pleased, for all he had to do was to warm up yesterday evening's stew in a double boiler.

When he went up to the second floor—going through the shop where, on Sunday, he did not light the gas— the Kachoudases were up. The sky was cloudless, a bluish green, footsteps were sounding in the street, and the clang of bells filled the city.

The little tailor, who had not yet washed his face and hands, had on a pair of trousers without suspenders over his nightshirt. Their Sundays always began with washing the children, to get them out of the way. But when they were ready, the difficulty was to keep them from getting their good clothes dirty.

The eldest, Esther, who worked at Prisunic, was walking about the rooms in her underwear, and Monsieur Labbé could make out the beginnings of her breasts. She was still thin, especially around the hips, but with rather too much bust than too little, like many girls of her age. Did she let her sweethearts paw her evening after evening in a dark corner of a doorway or a carriage gateway? Probably. It shocked Monsieur Labbé—he couldn't have said why—that men should get pleasure from Kachoudas' daughter, from flesh of the tribe of Kachoudas.

The little tailor, who wasn't looking well, didn't know what to do with himself. It was obvious that he was far from being his usual self. His conscience must be bothering him as much as his stomach. He took advantage of the day being Sunday to tidy up his workroom as usual, but he did it without any zest; his mind was elsewhere, and he more than once looked over at the house across the street, where the hatter was invisible behind the curtains.

What was the use of worrying about him? He'd keep

his mouth shut all right. He was terrified. Could a man like him go to the police and, in the accent he'd never lost, declare:

"The murderer you are looking for is my neighbor the hatter."

"Really?"

"I saw a scrap of paper at the bottom of his trousers, two letters cut out of a newspaper."

"Most interesting!"

"I followed him and he strangled Mademoiselle Irène Mollard right before my eyes."

"Think of that!"

"Then he said to me in the most natural voice:

" 'You'd be making a mistake, Kachoudas!' "

And it was true: he'd be making a mistake. Wouldn't it occur to them to ask him if he hadn't by any chance been wearing a beige raincoat? Wasn't it true that in every age and in every country on earth the Kachoudases were always the first to be suspected?

Enough of this—it was time to get to work! For what with having to cut out the letters, sometimes one by one, finding them in the articles, and pasting them so they fitted together, it was a slow process, even when you were used to it.

Monsieur Labbé never made a first draft. A ray of sunlight fell through the window and projected the elaborate flowers of the lace curtains onto the wall that faced him. In addition, two small disks of sunlight, which moved like living creatures, appeared to be playing a game on the mahogany of the desk.

In the Rue du Minage doors opened and closed, families made their way toward the church of Saint-Sauveur, between the canal and the port. Boat whistles sounded. Disregarding the fact that it was Sunday, the fishermen took advantage of the fog having lifted to put to sea, and they must be following one another in single file through the harbor channel.

The city was radiant, golden yellow in the sunshine; the harbor was an expanse of blue; soon the Kachoudases would be leaving their house, the children walking ahead in their good clothes, then Kachoudas and his wife, always a little awkward on Sunday, much less at their ease than on weekdays.

After mass they would stop in at the pastry shop in the Rue des Merciers, and it would be the little tailor who would carry the cardboard box by its red string on their way home.

Summary Notes on the Strangler's Victims.

He chose the word "Strangler" deliberately, not without a certain irony, because it was the word people used. Whether they understood or not didn't matter.

Before beginning, he stood on a chair, reached up with one hand, and brought down an object from the top of the wardrobe—a photograph in a narrow black wood frame. Two months earlier it had hung on the wall near Mathilde's bed; you could still see a lighter rectangle on the wallpaper.

It was a class photograph, taken at the Convent of the Immaculate Conception on a certain prize day.

It showed fifteen girls. Monsieur Labbé had often counted them, and he could put a name to each of the faces. They were all between sixteen and eighteen years old. They wore the same navy-blue uniform, a pleated skirt, hair in braids, and, around their necks, a ribbon from which hung a medal. In the center of the group was a thin, pale, ascetic nun, who looked like a religious picture and who had her hands hidden in her sleeves. To hear Mathilde tell it, she was a real bitch, despite her angelic smile.

The girls in the second row were standing on a sort of carpeted platform, and the whole group was framed by green plants.

With the photograph propped up in front of him against the copper inkstand—which was no longer of any

use, since he had a fountain pen—he went back to work, his tongue occasionally protruding between his lips.

Jacqueline Delobel, aged sixty, widow of an infantry **65**
captain.

She was the third from the left, a short brunette with a mischievous look and a pointed nose, who seemed to be trying hard to keep from laughing as she looked at the photographer, whose head must have been muffled in a black cloth.

Good family. Daughter of the notary Delobel, who wrote several books on local history. Lived with her husband in a number of garrison towns, among others Besançon. Had two children. A daughter, married to an importer in Marseilles, and a son, now a lieutenant of spahis. Lived alone in an apartment in the Rue des Merciers, above a rope and basket shop. Had quarreled with her daughter. Small private income. Would not accept money from her son, and sold her own needlework privately.

After thinking for a moment he added:

Her daughter did not attend the funeral. Her son, in garrison in Syria, was not notified in time.

That took care of the first one. She'd given him no trouble. Her health was poor. She stinted herself to make ends meet. In the evenings she used to trot around the city delivering her needlework; and in La Rochelle it is hard to get from one shopping street to another without passing through dark alleys.

Lucky that he'd begun on her. With a strong, healthy woman like Léonide Proux he might have botched it. For he hadn't yet thought up the idea of fastening two pieces of wood—like the ones some shopkeepers still put on packages by way of handles—to the two ends of the cello string.

Despite the slight resistance that Madame Delobel had made—or, indeed, the complete lack of resistance—he'd cut his fingers so deeply that they bled.

He'd very nearly made another mistake too. The thing had taken place not far from the canal, behind the church of Saint-Sauveur, and he'd thought of pushing the body into the canal. The tide was going out. The current was strong. Madame Delobel might not have been found until several days or several weeks later— perhaps never.

And that would have changed everything, for, later on, he couldn't have done the same with the other bodies. Mightn't it be said that the whole symmetry of the thing would have been destroyed? That would be going too far. But in any case it would have had quite a different character.

Afterward he'd been able to go to the Café des Colonnes and play a rubber, drinking his glass of Picon-grenadine.

Madame Cujas (Rosalie), bookseller, Rue des Merciers, wife of René Cujas, clerk at the town hall.

Another daughter of a good family, he was careful to record. He could simply have said that she'd been a pupil at the Immaculate Conception, which amounted to the same thing, but that would be dangerous. In any case, it was odd that no one had noticed that all the old women who'd been strangled during the last few weeks had been brought up in the same convent.

Only young Jeantet, who was intelligent, had observed that they were all about the same age, that they had a sort of family resemblance.

In the photograph the girl who had become Madame Cujas was probably the most beautiful, but it was a rather cold beauty.

Her father, he set down, *was deputy mayor of La Rochelle for twenty years.*

They were rich. She could have married anyone she chose. Why had she waited until she was twenty-eight before she married?

"She was too particular," Mathilde had said acidly, "she wouldn't settle for anything but true love."

And she added, but without bitterness:

"As if there were such a thing!"

At the age of twenty-eight she had married Cujas, for by that time her father had died, leaving his estate in such disorder that her brothers wanted to get rid of her in a hurry. Cujas had tried a dozen jobs before going to work at the town hall. He was not handsome. He was not especially intelligent. His health was poor, and it was his wife who kept the pot boiling.

Monsieur Labbé was well acquainted with the little bookstore, where, when he found nothing that interested him at the auction room, he would go and search through the two boxes of secondhand books that stood along the wall. It was not much of a bookstore. The principal sales were of postcards, fountain pens, pencils, erasers. But there was a back room, which was open only to regular customers and where some of his friends— Arnould of the sardine fleet, for example—found what they wanted in the way of erotic books.

He also knew that at the back of the establishment there was a door that opened onto a blind alley.

Since Madame Cujas had no maid, and never went out after the shop closed except occasionally to go to the movies with her husband, he could have waited months for a chance to catch her outdoors in the dark.

That was why he'd gone into the back room. The two pieces of wood on the ends of the cello string had proved to be extremely practical. She was more nervous than Madame Delobel. Once he was outside again, he'd even wondered if he had pulled long enough, and he hadn't felt reassured until the next day when he read the newspaper.

Once—it was ten or twelve years ago now—Mathilde had said to Madame Cujas, when they were talking about what had become of their old schoolmates:

"Life is no bed of roses."

And Madame Cujas had answered calmly:

"Why should it be?"

And that was what Monsieur Labbé had wanted to make people realize, but it was difficult. For each of them he had tried to find the right way to put it.

Considered life a trial, he pieced together from cut-out letters.

It wasn't to excuse himself. He had no need of excuses. It was more important than that, but he realized that the task he was accomplishing without letting himself be discouraged was very nearly impossible. A few nights earlier he'd had a strange dream, and it might have been because of that dream that he was working today. He had been in a big room that was like a parish hall, and all the prominent people in the city were sitting in the rows of chairs. He was on a platform, with a screen behind him and a long pointer in his hand, for he was giving a lecture with slides.

What was projected on the screen was the photograph taken long ago at the convent, and he pointed out the girls one by one.

He had begun, as if it were a matter of little importance, by a hasty elimination:

"We will say nothing of the ones who have died. . . ."

There were two of them. One had freckles and short curly hairs around her ears and along the hairline on her forehead, and had died of tuberculosis in a Swiss sanitarium at the age of twenty-two. The other, with eager eyes, already a woman while still in school, had married a big shipowner in La Rochelle and had died giving birth to her first child. The child was still alive. He had become a shipowner in his turn and lived in Bordeaux.

That left thirteen. One of them had lived in all the capitals of Europe with her husband, who was a consul;

they now resided in Turkey. Of yet another nothing was known except that she had left home at nineteen and that it had created a scandal. Her mother had died of it. Her father had married again.

That left eleven. The audience in the room listened without understanding much of what he was saying, and he did his best—but in vain—to make them grasp his thought. From time to time he would knock with his pointer on the floor of the platform, the slide in the projector would be changed, and a panoramic view of La Rochelle would appear—but such a view as did not exist, for you could see every street and every house and everyone in the streets, and, by some miracle, even the people inside their houses.

There was one of the young ladies who had been in the class at the convent who now lived in Paris, the wife of a minister, and whose daughter had married an Austrian aristocrat. Her picture often appeared in the newspapers; she had recently entered a hospital for an operation the nature of which had not been specified.

The Kachoudases had got home, and the children were already being undressed and dressed again in their everyday clothes. After lunch they would eat frosted cream buns with coffee. Kachoudas would change his clothes too and climb up on his table, unless he took advantage of its being Sunday to catch up on his accounts, always a difficult job.

It was the only day in the week that the whole family spent in the workroom, except Esther, whom some of her girl friends would come for before long, stopping under the windows and calling, through their cupped hands:

"Hi there!"

The tenth one . . . He was becoming a bit confused.

He ought to have taken notes when Mathilde was still there—she had it all at her fingertips. Let's see . . . There was one who was on the stage, not in Paris, but in a company that toured the provinces.

Two more . . . He pointed at the photograph with the end of his fountain pen as he had done with the pointer in his dream. The one who had had smallpox . . . She was forewoman in a dressmaking establishment in London and had come back to La Rochelle several times to see her mother, who was still alive and all shriveled up.

The last of the ones who had left the city was living in Lyon; that was all he knew about her.

That left seven, besides Mathilde, and that accounted for them all, since the nun in the photograph, whose name was Mother Sainte Josephine, was out of the question—she had died long ago.

Mademoiselle Anne-Marie Lange, dry goods, Rue Saint-Yon.

The Kachoudases were at the table. After this one, he'd go and eat lunch himself. He'd have all afternoon for the rest of them.

A fat old maid who stuffed herself with pastries and kept her house full of cats. She was blond and pink, always dressed in light colors, with a high-pitched voice and singsong inflections.

Good family. Her father . . .

Her father ran after young working girls, and it had gotten him into trouble; there'd been scandals that had had to be hushed up. At the age of seventy-five, he was still at it, and his family had to keep an eye on him, follow him when he went out; they didn't let him have any pocket money at all and they'd dismissed the maids, keeping only menservants in the house. Now he was dead. One of his daughters was in America. Anne-Marie, who had never married, lived in her shop with a

retired schoolmistress whose manner was dictatorial, and scandalmongers insisted that the two of them got on very well together without men.

It might have been true. For her, in any case, the way to put it was easy. He had only to say what the newspapers had said.

The autopsy revealed the presence of a fibroma and a tumor which would probably have become cancerous.

It had been raining so hard on Mademoiselle Lange's day that he'd been able to attack her in the middle of the Rue Gargoulleau, only a step or two from the Hôtel de France. Her arms were loaded with little packages, which had scattered over the sidewalk, among them a bottle of cream, which had broken.

It was time to eat lunch. He went downstairs, warmed up his stew, threw part of it into the toilet bowl, since he couldn't always eat for two. On Sunday he didn't have to take the tray upstairs, and that was so much to the good. Afterward he washed the dishes.

"You could leave them, and I'll do them when I get back," Louise had suggested.

And so he could have done. But he didn't like things left lying around, especially dirty dishes. Then too, it gave him something to do. It was part of the Sunday ritual.

He went upstairs again, washed his hands thoroughly. Across the street the Kachoudas children were playing on the floor. Madame Kachoudas was busily darning woolen socks, and the tailor was trying to do his accounts, wetting his pencil with saliva now and again and asking his wife a question:

"What's seven plus nine?"

Sometimes Monsieur Labbé would take a nap in his armchair, an armchair upholstered in crimson velvet like Mathilde's, but today his work excited him. He was nearing the end. Tomorrow night, if all went well, he

would have finished. He felt impatient, yet at the same time foresaw an emptiness.

Afterward he would only have to think of little details which had become routine and which no longer exercised his mind.

Up to now he had not made a single mistake: he was sure that he wouldn't make any. Even the accident that had happened with the little tailor had no significance. It didn't frighten him. On the contrary. He was almost glad of it. Could it be that, until then, he'd been too alone?

With Louise, it had been deliberately that he'd taken certain risks.

From now on, there was someone who knew, and that was perfect. Kachoudas would read his statement in the *Écho des Charentes.*

Would he understand certain things now?

Madame Geoffroy-Lambert, widow of the president of the Equalization Fund . . .

Justine! That was what everybody called the sister of his friend Julien Lambert, the insurance agent. He'd gone to her funeral. He'd gone to all the funerals, for they were all for people he knew.

Another widow. There were a lot of widows. It was true that Justine had married a man twenty years older than herself, a prominent, wealthy man who owned the finest private house in the city, in the Rue Réaumur, and another in Paris, where he spent most of the year.

He was one of those high officials whose duties remain a mystery to the common run of mankind. He had begun in the treasury. A minister without portfolio, he was said to have been the most cuckolded man in France.

After his death, in any case, Justine was supposed to have had an inordinate love for young men. In her house there was hard drinking and dancing till dawn, and at the

age of sixty she showed not the slightest intention of
giving up the game.

She had a chauffeur who was said to be her lover; but
to visit the shops in the Rue du Palais—where, with her
shrill voice, she carried on more or less like a queen—
she had only a short way to go and she did it on foot.
Fortunately!

She was the one who had given him the most trouble.
She'd had an umbrella up, and a rib of it had almost put
out one of his eyes when he flung himself on her. He'd
caught her under the chin with the cello string, and
she'd struggled, had kicked him, and to such effect that
he'd been almost on the point of running away without
finishing the thing.

He'd managed it nevertheless; it was the only time
he'd had to run, for a door had opened less than thirty
feet away; he still seemed to hear a man's voice saying
politely:

"Thank you, Madame. I'll certainly keep it in mind. I
can assure you that if it had been my responsibility you
would have been satisfied long ago."

No doubt a contractor's representative, or somebody
of that sort.

Justine wasn't ill. She wasn't unhappy or resigned.
She didn't have the slightest wish to pass into the other
world. For example, the hatter found it hard to bring
himself to write:

Is she a loss to society?

Not even to her family, who lived in fear of a possible
scandal, and so much so that her daughter, married to a
prominent man, forbade her to set foot in Paris.

After summarizing her *curriculum vitae* he let it go at
adding a question mark.

Léonide Proux, age sixty-one, midwife, from Fé-
tilly . . .

The Proux family had owned twenty farms and two

country houses, and Léonide had been reduced to living in Fétilly, a suburb of the city, close to the gasworks and inhabited by railwaymen, clerks, and factory hands.

Was it true that her father, who had lost his fortune in wild speculations, was actually mad, as some people claimed? Was it true that her husband, dead at forty-one, was syphilitic? In any case, a deformed daughter had died in childhood, and their son was not like other people; in spite of that he had married and now lived on his parents-in-law, who cultivated a small vineyard in the Dordogne.

As long as he lived Proux slept out half the time. He would even come home with women he'd picked up God knows where, sometimes in the district around the barracks, and one night he'd beaten Léonide in front of them on the pretext that he couldn't stand seeing her crying and that she cried on purpose to make his life unbearable.

She'd been obliged to support herself. She had learned midwifery at the hospital. She was calm and cold; she was said to be very good at her profession. No one had ever seen her laugh or smile, and she had a way of grabbing newborn infants by the feet that froze their mothers' blood.

The difficulty was to convey all that, and what it meant, in a few sentences, for he couldn't go on forever cutting letters out of the newspaper.

It was not true that he'd telephoned to her. He'd got her by chance, when he'd gone to lurk around her house learning her comings and goings. He'd even hesitated to bring his cello string. The house was very small, with a light above the door.

Léonide had come out when he'd been there only a few minutes, and she was carrying her bag of instruments. He'd followed her as far as the gasworks. He'd waited for an automobile to pass. She'd recognized him,

had had time to turn her head, but it was too late. She had shown neither surprise nor fear. He didn't dare write that she had been relieved, though it was not far from the truth.

As for Irène Mollard, he'd written what he needed to say to the newspaper the next morning. Both in the photograph and when she'd come out from giving her last piano lesson, she made him think of a bird fallen from the nest. It was a miracle she had lived so long.

There was only one left, Armandine d'Hautebois, now Mother Sainte-Ursule, who in other photographs of prize days with other girls played in her turn the part played long ago by Mother Sainte-Josephine.

She had, so to speak, passed directly from the photograph to the convent. She hadn't gone to the trouble of living or even of attempting it, yet she was rich, she had brothers and sisters who had made their mark in the world.

He would see to it tomorrow, for she left the convent of the Immaculate Conception only once a month, the second Monday, to go to the bishop's palace. She wouldn't be alone. Nuns never go out alone. She would have no more than fifty yards to get through the darkness, and Monsieur Labbé had had to put together a quite complicated plan.

Would Kachoudas follow him again? At bottom, the hatter hoped that he would.

If things happened exactly as he foresaw, tomorrow at six o'clock it would all be finished and done with.

He didn't want to think about Louise. It was absurd to be tempted. It didn't fit in with anything.

Several times, as he went to put logs on the fire, then to let down the blind, for night had fallen, he repeated to himself:

"Above all, not Louise!"

He went downstairs and poured himself a glass of
brandy, of which he kept a bottle in the dining-room
cupboard. He sat down to drink it slowly, sip by sip,
after putting the bottle away again so that he wouldn't be
tempted to take a second glass.

5

There were all sorts of little things that displeased him, irritated him, and it had begun in the morning. Valentin had come to work half an hour late, with bandage around his neck and his eyes bright with fever; his head cold had got so much worse that he didn't take time to put his handkerchief back in his pocket. The clerk had literally flowed all day long; you could see him liquefying, and his voice was so hoarse you could scarcely understand what he said.

The hatter ought to have sent him home. The young fellow's mother probably thought he was a brute to keep him at work in such a state. Valentin himself had expected to be let off. And the worst thing was that Monsieur Labbé felt sorry for him. He could see very well that the poor boy was sometimes dizzy.

"Have you taken aspirin, Valentin?"

"Yes, sir."

"Are there white spots in your throat?"

"No, sir. Mother looked again this morning. My throat's very red, but there aren't any spots."

So much the better; Monsieur Labbé was susceptible to catching a sore throat, and this was not the time. Valentin's cold was all the more ridiculous because it wasn't raining; the sky was transparently clear. It is true that it was so chilly until nine in the morning that the breaths of people in the streets made little patches of fog.

When he went to buy his newspaper he brought back some menthol-flavored cough drops for Valentin. Two

or three times that morning he said to him from back in the workroom:

"Take a little rest. Don't stay over there by the show window. Get close to the fire."

Near the windows the air was frigid.

Louise was worrying him too. The night before, she had come in at nine o'clock as usual and then she'd got into what he called her ornery mood. It was periodic. Did it coincide with certain functions of her organism? Yet he'd noticed that it usually followed one of her visits to Charron.

Somebody there must put ideas into her head—her parents, a sweetheart, a girl friend. Monsieur Labbé paid her well. He hadn't haggled over the salary she'd asked. He let her eat whatever she chose. He rarely criticized her. Despite all that, she had something in the back of her mind; did she bear him a grudge? Who could have guessed what went on behind that stubborn forehead of hers.

You could tell she was in that kind of a mood just from her footsteps, the way she moved things about.

What harm could it do the hatter?

To make up for these little annoyances, he had dropped his statement into the box in the main post office, and he had found, on the front page of the paper, an announcement that had been emphasized by a box.

The mayor of La Rochelle, officer of the Légion d'Honneur, urgently requests all citizens to be more cautious than ever during the evening of Monday, December 12. Doubtless from sheer bravado, the individual who has been terrorizing the city for more than a month and who has already killed six victims has announced another murder for today. We ask especially that ladies do not go out after nightfall and that mothers keep their children indoors.

The city government will make arrangements to have

all female employees in offices, shops, and factories escorted home.

The present patrols will be reinforced.

He looked across the street; there was nothing worth noting in the house opposite: Kachoudas had begun working feverishly; he scarcely even looked up.

Was that all? Another detail: since three o'clock that afternoon, when the sky was turning a soft pink, you could already see a big silvery moon.

But then, that evening, Kachoudas didn't behave in his usual way.

"You can shut up the shop, Valentin."

"Yes, sir."

A glance at the other house. He lingered purposely. The little tailor finally left, but not until the hatter had already gone a hundred yards. On other evenings he didn't wait as long as that.

Monsieur Labbé entered the Café des Colonnes, shook hands with Chantreau, Caillé, Laude, and Oscar, the proprietor.

"I took a hand while we were waiting for you," said the latter, rising.

"I haven't time to play today."

"One rubber, Léon," the doctor urged him.

"Mathilde has a cold. I promised her I'd come right home."

What was Kachoudas doing? The door of the café didn't open. The other times, he'd come in soon after Monsieur Labbé. It irritated the hatter. Gabriel, as always, had offered to take his overcoat, and he hadn't let him, because the weight of the piece of lead pipe would betray its presence in the right-hand pocket.

"I can stay only a few minutes."

It was Laude who joked, stupidly:

"It seems you're afraid of the murderer too! If this keeps up, the whole city will become hysterical."

What on earth could Kachoudas be doing? He was behind him when he'd turned the corner of the Rue du Minage.

He drank down his Picon-grenadine.

"One rubber," Chantreau begged again. "Just long enough for a fourth to get here."

He had to refuse. The time had come to leave. The paving stones were almost white under the moon, which cast shadows as sharply cut as sheet metal.

It was the first time he'd felt nervous. He had the inpression that, now that he'd left, the men in the café were talking about him. Saying what? He crossed the center of the Place d'Armes to take the Rue Réaumur, and it was not till then that he heard footsteps behind him, turned, and saw the figure of the little tailor.

So he'd deliberately changed his behavior. He hadn't gone to the café. Having read, like everybody else, that the murderer would attack his seventh victim that day, he had suspected that the hatter would make only a brief appearance at the Colonnes. Did he want to avoid leaving directly after him another time—which would eventually be noticed?

Then too, mightn't he have run into someone just as he was entering the café—Pigeac, for example? It wasn't likely. Pigeac probably wouldn't go to the café that evening. He must be at his headquarters, directing both the reinforced police and the patrols of volunteers.

Monsieur Labbé passed the departmental office building, entered the small square in front of the bishop's palace, and had nothing left to do but wait. The old building of gray stone showed lights here and there. Kachoudas cautiously waited fifty yards away from him.

The hatter's nerves were strained to the point that he almost gave it up and went home, but he couldn't reappear at the café after what he'd said about Mathilde having caught a cold.

He had the depressing feeling that he'd been the

victim of an injustice. He'd done all that he could. For weeks he hadn't allowed himself a respite, he'd thought of everything, of the most paltry details. Thanks to that, to the trouble he'd taken, he had succeeded, without a hitch.

He was reaching his goal. This evening everything was to be finished. He had ungrudgingly accepted an extra risk, for Mother Sainte-Ursule would be accompanied by another nun. It was for her that he intended the lead pipe. He would hit her quickly, hard enough to stun her, and that would give him time to dispatch the former Armandine d'Hautebois. With her voluminous pleated habit, she could hardly start running. And he couldn't imagine her screaming at the top of her voice, either.

It was delicate, difficult. It demanded precision and coolness. Yesterday evening he still thought about it with a certain pleasure, imagined the little tailor's presence without any nervousness.

Why, ever since this morning, had he felt as if there were some sort of conspiracy against him? The middle of the square was as white as milk. A patrol passed through the street, and he made out the shape of a fishmonger who stayed drunk all the time and was famous for his brutality.

Normally, the two nuns ought to be in the bishop's palace at this time. It was Mother Sainte-Ursule's day. She never missed it. Not only had Mathilde told him so; he had made sure of it himself a month ago.

The last time, she had left the bishop's palace at a quarter before six. And a quarter before six had already struck. It was very nearly six, and not a light changed in the stone building, not a sound was to be heard. Monsieur Labbé stared in vain at the door that didn't open, while from time to time Kachoudas stamped his feet to warm himself.

The hatter's feet were cold too. And suddenly his

thoughts focused on Mother Sainte-Ursule. Hadn't she noticed that all the strangler's victims were former classmates of hers?

Didn't she read the newspaper? If she didn't, people must talk to her about the case. The names were well known to her. That it hadn't occurred to the others to make the connection could be explained in one way or another. But Mother Sainte-Ursule?

It was getting close to December 24. That date must inevitably revive her memories.

He couldn't go and ring at the bishop's palace, ask if the nun was there. The minutes passed. Six o'clock struck. What was Kachoudas thinking all this time? For he was thinking. Monsieur Labbé even had the feeling that he'd started thinking in a new way. The proof was his new behavior.

He wanted his twenty thousand francs—that was only human. If he was following the hatter, it was because he hoped the hatter would make some mistake, would give him some proof that would enable him to go and claim the reward.

But exactly what convolutions did his thoughts follow? That was what Monsieur Labbé would have liked to know. The bishop's palace, for example? What did that suggest to the little fellow from the Near East?

Mother Sainte-Ursule did not appear. Very likely she wasn't there. She hadn't left the convent. It didn't much matter whether it was out of caution or for some other reason. The bishop might have been away; but that wasn't so, for Monsieur Labbé read the newspaper carefully and the bishop's travels were regularly announced in it.

The truth was probably something more commonplace. Like Valentin, the nun might have caught a cold, have a sore throat.

He couldn't just stay there indefinitely. He waited

until quarter past six and then left, overcome by a feeling of apprehension that was not only anxiety.

To tell the truth, it was not anxiety at all. It was of no consequence what Kachoudas thought. He'd given him one end of a thread—yes. The little tailor's mind would work on this clue of the bishop's palace. For someone who'd spent his childhood in the city, and even more for someone who'd had a sister in the convent, it could, strictly speaking, lead to something.

That wasn't true of a poor Armenian workman. Monsieur Labbé had no fear of Kachoudas. He didn't fear anyone. The proof was that he'd purposely made his task more difficult and more dangerous by announcing that his seventh victim would die on this Monday.

He didn't want to go home earlier than usual because of Louise. She couldn't think, either—he was sure of that; but he didn't want to leave anything to chance, he didn't want to see astonishment in the wench's empty eyes.

He passed under the clock tower and took advantage of there being no one about to throw the lead pipe into the water of the harbor. On the waterfront quantities of little cafés were open, bars chiefly patronized by fishermen; he wanted to go into one of them, have a drink, and he had to restrain himself.

He wasn't afraid. It was more complicated and more disturbing. The other times—even the time when Kachoudas had seen what he did—he'd been sure of himself, his whole being had, as it were, been pervaded by waves of self-confidence, of assuagement.

Kachoudas was taking care to remain at a safe distance. Perhaps today he was not so wrong to be cautious —who knows?

It was idiotic. Monsieur Labbé didn't want to give in to such ideas; yet he couldn't manage to dismiss them entirely. He began thinking up arguments against them.

"However terrified he is, Kachoudas will certainly end by talking."

First of all, that was not certain. If he'd had friends, maybe. But he was alone; the Kachoudases were something like a foreign body in the city. He didn't play cards with anyone, didn't belong to any group, any organization. There were no other people of his race in La Rochelle. They lived by themselves, with their cooking, their habits, their smell.

What good would it do to do away with him instead of with Mother Sainte-Ursule? Then too, he'd start running like a rabbit as soon as Monsieur Labbé made a move toward him.

What had put that idea into his head? He was walking along the sidewalk, with his hands in his pockets, when a patrol passed him; the pork butcher from across the street, who was one of them, spoke to him politely:

"Good evening, Monsieur Labbé."

He passed by the canal, just where he had attacked Madame Delobel, and he had the nostalgic feeling of a time gone beyond recall; it nearly overcame him.

Was he going to become soft, uneasy, hesitant? It was more physical than moral, like certain states of tiredness that suddenly seize you, like flu.

After all, couldn't it be that Valentin had flu and Monsieur Labbé had caught it from him? He found the idea consoling. He was not very far from the convent of the Immaculate Conception, and he wondered once again why Mother Sainte-Ursule hadn't gone out. Kachoudas was still following him at a distance, and the hatter thought he would very much have liked to speak to him.

He was the only man that day with whom he could have talked. He had seen him in action. He knew. But how did he interpret his acts?

It went without saying that he was incapable of understanding. Neither he nor anyone else would understand,

and that was another of the things that troubled him. If Kachoudas had a flash of genius, could he perhaps, by starting off from the bishop's palace, arrive at the truth? Especially Kachoudas, who for so many years had seen the form of Mathilde, motionless behind the curtain, and the hatter's comings and goings in the bedroom.

The pork butcher had almost the same view. However, he seldom went up to the third floor except to go to bed, and after eight o'clock in the evening he was always half drunk anyway.

Louise? The slut didn't have a brain in her head. He hated her. Every day he hated her more, without any particular reason. She was in his house like a splinter under one of his fingernails: her mere presence was enough to cause him physical pain.

He passed Madame Cujas' bookstore, where the widow had taken on a young girl to wait at the counter. She cooked the meals for the clerk at the town hall and slept in the house. Before long they would be sleeping together.

Monsieur Labbé thought of Mademoiselle Berthe and felt sorry that he couldn't go and see her. It was impossible that day. It was too late. He'd told his friends that he had to get home early because of his wife.

He'd pay her a visit tomorrow. It would be amusing if Kachoudas waited at the door in the Rue Gargoulleau while he went to it with her.

But . . . luckily he thought of everything. He was the first to be surprised by it. There were so many details to consider, so many possibilities to foresee, that he could have been excused for forgetting something.

He suddenly realized that he could no longer go to Mademoiselle Berthe's, as he was in the habit of doing once or twice a month. Because of Kachoudas! He wouldn't put it beyond the little tailor to fall into a panic, imagine that he was going to strangle the woman, and run and tell the police.

Kachoudas was a hindrance, and yet he still needed him. Even the sound of his footsteps behind him had come to be almost indispensable.

He turned the corner of the Rue du Minage, feeling more and more depressed and at the same time trying to determine why, and the irritation that it caused was becoming anxiety.

The other times, he'd had such a feeling of fulfillment when he arrived near his house!

He wouldn't have admitted it to anyone, not even to Kachoudas, who knew; today he felt something like guilt. The feeling that a man has who has failed to accomplish a task that he'd set himself.

Someday, perhaps, he'd talk to the tailor, whom he could never strangle. First, he wasn't on his list. Second, he lived across the street, and it might occur to people to think of the hatter.

He took his bunch of keys from his pocket, carefully closed and relocked the door, fastened the bolt. It was hot inside; the shop still smelled of eucalyptus, which was, as it were, the smell of Valentin's cold.

"Has Madame called?"

"No, sir."

Had Louise noticed that her mistress, whom she had never seen, never called when Monsieur Labbé was away? What could she be telling her relatives, her girl friends on her Sundays off?

She was boiling cabbage. She knew perfectly well that he didn't like cabbage and yet she served it. She was like that. When he pointed it out to her, she looked at him stolidly and said nothing, made no excuses.

She liked cabbage herself!

He took off his overcoat, his hat, put the cello string into the hollow of the wooden head at the far end of the back room. Then he started up the spiral staircase, and he still felt sad, without zest, out of spirits.

It made him more and more uneasy. He did every-thing that he had to do, went through the ritual scrupu-lously: the blind, the armchair, then the dinner he had to throw into the toilet bowl and flush down. He didn't forget to speak in a low voice, and when he went down-stairs again he looked at Louise with hatred; the tempta-tion was so strong that he nearly went back into the workroom for the cello string.

Luckily, he got over it. That was the last thing he ought to do. Especially in his own house! Especially with that family of suspicious peasants ready to come down on him.

"Has nobody come in?" he asked, regaining his self-possession.

"No."

She seemed to be saying:

"What's the use of asking me that, since nobody ever comes?"

Nobody. Never for years and years. Because every-one in the city knew that Mathilde couldn't bear the presence of a human being, except her husband, and that the least unusual sound in the house threw her into a spasm of terror.

Despite himself, he still lingered in the dining room, sometimes looking sidewise at the fat stupid wench, and he ended by opening the buffet and taking out the bottle of brandy. Too bad about what she might think! Too bad for him too—because taking this step, going upstairs with the bottle in one hand and a glass in the other, only made him still more uneasy, increased his feeling of guilt.

He never drank spirits in the evening, after his dinner. Why was he doing so today? It troubled him even more, when he pushed the curtain aside, not to see Kachoudas in his place on the table, for the tailor had had plenty of time to finish dining. He couldn't see him

anywhere in the room. As if by chance, the door to the kitchen was shut. What was he up to? Had he shut himself in to tell his wife what he knew?

Monsieur Labbé simply must get back his self-control. He was even more put out with himself when he nearly gulped a drink of brandy right from the bottle, and he forced himself to walk over to his desk, fill his glass slowly, and empty it by little sips.

When he went back to the window and moved the curtain aside again, Kachoudas was there. He looked as if he had never left his place—and so much so that the hatter wondered if he'd looked thoroughly enough earlier.

It ought all to have been finished at this hour. Again and again he had promised himself that relief! He'd been thinking of it for weeks, day after day!

And now nothing was finished. Mother Sainte-Ursule was alive in her convent. Had she by any chance also kept the prize-day photograph? She had only to happen to look at that photograph, and she would understand. Suddenly he stood stock still in the middle of the room, and every sign of strain vanished from his face, his muscles relaxed. Actually, he merely smiled, but it came to the same thing.

You believe you've thought of everything, you do your best to forget nothing, and there's one tiny little thing that you fail to take into account.

It was because of the photograph. He'd begun by basing everything on the photograph. It was by the help of it that he'd made up his list. The photograph had continued to govern his strategy and his actions as well as his thoughts.

Why had he been in such a hurry as even to do away with two women in one week, if not because of December 24?

But Mother Sainte-Ursule had never set foot in the hat shop either on December 24 or on any other date.

There must have been something that prohibited her doing it. Hadn't Mathilde said that, even when her mother was dying, she hadn't been allowed to enter her house?

She had merely sent a religious picture, with a letter four pages long, written in a delicate regular hand, and which inevitably ended with:

". . . I pray to God to have you in His Holy Keeping."

So what followed? He hadn't thought of that, and had gone to a lot of useless trouble. He'd wasted his time hanging about in front of the bishop's palace.

There was no reason at all to put Mother Sainte-Ursule on the list!

Had there been other things of the kind that had escaped him? He felt uneasy again, put some logs on the fire, went back to the window, made certain that the little tailor was in his place, and through the half-open door at the back of the room saw Madame Kachoudas washing children's clothes in the kitchen sink.

He must go over it all again from the beginning, but he wasn't up to doing it this evening. He'd just drunk three glasses of brandy one after the other, and he felt ashamed.

He bitterly remembered the last few weeks, when he'd felt so sure of himself, when he was so superior to everyone else.

Louise came shuffling up the staircase and, as usual, made a racket on the landing, and Monsieur Labbé's fingers tightened as they would have liked to tighten around her neck.

It would be enough to get him caught. He was almost certain to be caught if he let himself indulge in that. And afterward? Wouldn't it give him just the opportunity to explain everything to them?

He took another drink. He didn't even pick up his book. He ought to have been peacefully absorbed in the trial of the Jura agitator a good half hour ago.

What had he gone to the trouble of stating in his letters to the newspaper, not once but several times, emphatically, at the risk of setting the police or young Jeantet on his trail?

That it was a matter of necessity.

He had told them, in short:

"You call me a lunatic, a maniac, a man with an obsession [they had even brought up the idea of a sex maniac, though none of the old women had been raped]. You are wrong. I am a man of completely sound mind. If my acts seem abnormal to you, it is because you do not know all the facts. And unfortunately, concern for my personal safety prevents me from giving you the necessary information. You would understand then. There are seven women on the list, and I did not pick that number by chance. I am acting logically, because it is necessary. You will realize it when the seventh woman is dead. After that, nothing will happen. La Rochelle will again be as peaceful as ever."

He had not killed the seventh one. The newspaper would announce the fact tomorrow morning. And because of that, no one would believe him any longer. Not only had he not killed the seventh one, he had just discovered that the death of Mother Sainte-Ursule would be one too many.

What would people think? That he wrote anything at all, just to make himself interesting? That he took his victims at random?

That he'd been afraid? That the mayor's announcement had produced its effect?

He had on his slippers and his dressing gown, as on other evenings. He lighted his meerschaum pipe, the one he usually smoked at that hour and that had a different taste from the others, sat down in his armchair with his book, but kept the bottle of brandy within reach. That was enough to tell him that something had gone wrong.

If he'd come to feel a certain fondness for young Jeantet, it was because the young man gave him an opportunity to discuss his own case. It was a real controversy that they'd engaged in in the columns of the *Écho des Charentes*, both of them always looking for fresh arguments.

Jeantet had even gone all the way to Bordeaux to ask a well-known psychiatrist for his opinion, and after long scientific considerations the psychiatrist had predicted:

"He will not stop till he gets caught."

He had added, after thinking for a moment (Jeantet had emphasized this):

"Unless he commits suicide."

The hatter had replied confidently:

"I will not be caught. I will not commit suicide. I have no reason to do so. When the seventh person on the list is out of the way, the thing will be over."

He had repeated:

"It is a *necessity*."

It was no longer a necessity to kill the seventh one, because Mother Sainte-Ursule never set foot in the house in the Rue du Minage on December 24.

So, according to what he himself had announced—except for one slight change—it was finished. He had only to relax. He could go on playing cat and mouse with Kachoudas, who would be completely at a loss to understand it when he saw him from now on living a perfectly normal life.

He would keep on following him every day, spying on him at the Café des Colonnes.

A patrol passed down the street, three or four men whose footsteps rang on the frozen pavement. There were perhaps twenty patrols going about the city. The volunteers relieved one another, took turns getting warm at the big stove in the police station. The mayor remained in his office, where negative reports were telephoned to him. Jeantet stayed at the printing plant,

near the presses, which would soon start rolling, so that he could write a short article just at press time.

Monsieur Labbé jumped up from his chair, his nerves on edge. It was too much—the absolute stillness of the room, the air so stagnant that it was almost solid; he was ready to act, to do no matter what.

He'd made a mistake when he'd begun drinking, and now he had to keep on with it. Otherwise he might find himself going out, even taking the length of cello string and the two pieces of wood with him. Was it possible he'd do that?

He heard the bedspring creak in the maid's room, and his hatred for the fat wench grew so intense that she became almost pitiable.

He thought it would calm him to pick up his scissors, the newspapers from which he cut letters; he opened the paste pot and put a blank sheet of paper in front of him.

He would tell them . . .

Tell them what? He sat there with his scissors in the air, and for the first time in years he suddenly wanted to cry. He had a painful feeling that fate had played him a scurvy trick. He'd done too much—straightforwardly, bravely. He had arranged everything; by dint of patience, of prudence, he had thought of everything; he . . .

This evening it was all to be finished, and nothing was finished. Everyone would laugh at him, and everyone would be right.

It wasn't the little tailor across the street who was troubling him, with his grubby intelligence that would get nowhere. Neither was it the aristocratic and haughty Mother Sainte-Ursule in the peace of her convent.

He wasn't afraid of anyone—that's what they ought to have been telling themselves, the whole lot of them, and Inspector Pigeac first of all, and the mayor, who thought

he was so important, and young Jeantet along with them.

Nobody frightened him.

Except himself. For he was beginning to understand what had happened to him a while ago, when he was walking along the Quai Duperré. At first he'd thought that his anger had been due to the nun's having left him in the lurch by failing to show up at the bishop's palace.

After that his uneasiness had only increased, and for a moment he had thought of substituting the little tailor for Mother Sainte-Ursule.

That proved he had made a mistake.

Why, after that, had he hung around Louise?

It hadn't been the first time, he realized now. He'd already said to himself sometimes when he looked at her:

"How about afterward, when I've finished with the others?"

He drank. He needed a drink. He felt a kind of vertigo. What he seemed to glimpse was terrifying. He thought that he could regain his self-possession, force himself to think more calmly, by going to get the photograph, but those girlish faces, all frozen into the same artificial expression, no longer awoke any response in him.

That bitch of a Louise wasn't asleep, kept turning heavily from side to side in her bed, as if she sensed some danger in the house.

She needn't worry! He wouldn't do anything to her. He was calm. He was becoming calm again. He just needed to think, but there was no use trying to do it today. He'd drunk. Too bad. He'd better just go on, drink himself into a stupor, so he could sleep heavily, and tomorrow he'd be his old self again.

Then he'd prove to them that his mind was as sane as his body was sound. There was nothing wrong with him;

he'd made sure of it more than once by consulting eminent doctors. His father had died of a bad heart at the age of seventy-two, in full possession of his faculties. He was a hatter, in the same house, in the same street, at a time when the Rue du Minage was one of the principal shopping streets in the city, and he was a prominent man, a member of the city council.

The son had begun to study law at Poitiers, and it was of his own free will that in his third year of law school he had decided to go back to the hat shop.

It was entirely his own doing; no one else had had anything to say about it.

He was in perfect health.

There was still a light in Kachoudas' house, but the little tailor was no longer on his table. He stood leaning against it, smoking a cigarette he had just rolled and talking quietly with his wife, who had sat down for a moment.

Monsieur Labbé had no intention of being influenced by anybody.

"Let them say what they please, think and write what they please!"

He had drunk nearly half the bottle and he was beginning to understand. It had not been by chance that this or that had been printed about him. It was all part of a preconceived plan. Their idea was to drive him to distraction, to play havoc with his nerves so they'd be more certain to catch him.

Jeantet, the mayor, Pigeac, and even his friend Caillé were all in it together. They had a plan. Could the interview with the Bordeaux psychiatrist have been a fake? Or had they let him into the plot too?

Louise could toss back and forth on her creaking bed till it made her sick; he wouldn't stir.

He'd go to bed right away. What was there that he still had to do? He mustn't forget anything. His head was

heavy. It would be stupid to have caught Valentin's flu; he'd have done better to send him home to his mother.

He returned the photograph to its place, put away the scissors and the newspapers, put the stopper back in the paste pot.

He'd failed with Mother Sainte-Ursule. Well, that was that. Since she never came on December 24, it didn't matter in the least.

So he *had* finished.

That was what he must keep telling himself. He had finished. He need only go to sleep, drink a last swig of brandy if need be—and this time he drank it from the bottle.

Had he deserved it or hadn't he?

Finished.

No matter what they do!

Then why did he hug his pillow convulsively, like a child going to cry?

He went through every motion, forgot nothing. But more and more often he would find himself brought up stock still, as if in a trance, staring about him, first with a look of uneasiness, then of sorrow. His forehead would become creased. Once Valentin offered to help him.

"Did you forget something?"

Monsieur Labbé had looked at him as some creature not of this planet must look at human beings, without bothering to answer. He had scarcely even shrugged his shoulders. A few seconds later contact had been re-established. He knew again what he had to do, and he had gone to the closet at the back, the one that was kept locked, to pull the string.

On Tuesday morning he was pale, his features looked blurred, his eyelids red. It had been a very long time since he had let himself drink as he had drunk the evening before, and his head was empty, his fingers had trembled as he shaved.

The absurd thing was that, of the two of them, it was the little tailor who was really ill. Was it serious? Monsieur Labbé couldn't know that yet. He guessed from the most insignificant comings and goings in the house that something unusual was happening. It had been Madame Kachoudas who had appeared first. Then, much earlier than usual, Esther had come out of the kitchen fully dressed.

It is strange to see how easily, once its ritual is interrupted, a house takes on a look of catastrophe. The girl had gone downstairs, had spent quite a time unfastening

the bolts of the shop door, then had walked off down the sidewalk.

There was a slippery film of hoarfrost on the pavements that morning. How had Monsieur Labbé known at once that she was going to the pharmacy? Probably because nothing but illness or death can keep men like Kachoudas from their duty.

His wife was hurrying on the little girls, who were getting dressed for school. Esther must have gone to several pharmacies before she found one that was open. When she came back she was carrying a package, and as she was on her way upstairs Kachoudas, despite his wife's protests, appeared in the workroom. He was in slippers, with an old pair of trousers and an old jacket over his nightshirt and a black shawl that belonged to his wife around his neck. He showed plainly that he had a fever, and from the way he spoke it was also clear, even from across the street, that he'd lost his voice.

They opened the package from the pharmacy. Esther gave voluble explanations. A thermometer was produced, and Madame Kachoudas put it into her husband's mouth, then she carefully read the instructions on a bottle and on a small box. They helped the invalid put on his overcoat, not because he wanted to go out but because, despite the fire burning in the stove, he was beginning to shiver.

All three of them looked serious when they read the thermometer. They argued. The wife and daughter must have been proposing that they call the doctor, and Kachoudas would have none of it. Esther left to go to work. Her mother saw the two little girls out to the sidewalk, and they started off for school, hand in hand. The youngest had on a knitted cap of coarse red wool and gloves of the same color.

"Just the two of us now," Madame Kachoudas seemed to say as she returned to her husband.

She put water on to heat, got compresses ready, made

him swallow some pills that were presumably purgative. The little tailor, with nothing to do, looked longingly at his worktable, and as soon as he was left alone seemed to want to get up from the wicker armchair in which he'd been made to sit near the stove.

He must have a cold or a sore throat, like Valentin, who was still constantly blowing his nose.

Had Louise really felt afraid of the hatter when he had gone into the dining room just as she was setting the table? When she'd raised her head, a trifle suddenly, she'd seemed surprised to see him there near her, and after a silence, instead of saying good morning to him, she'd asked:

"What's wrong with you?"

What was wrong was that he had a hangover for sure, but more especially that he was looking at her with new eyes. He wasn't only looking at her, he was smelling her, overcome by an immense disgust, by a resentment that he could never again shake off. How many times, last evening, had he been tempted to go down to the kitchen, and then, later on when she'd gone to bed, to follow her into her room and finish with her?

Now he saw her, weighed her, measured her. He imagined her on the floor, and it nauseated him; he hated her, he would hate her for all eternity because of what he had nearly done to her.

It reminded him of his first erotic experiences, when he'd been about seventeen years old. He had resisted for a long time before he'd taken the plunge into the district around the barracks, where there were five or six brothels with women on the doorsteps. He'd begun by hurrying past, then, at the end of the street, making a detour that brought him back to where he could start along it again. Each time he promised himself he would choose, yet he always ended by going into some random hallway, with his ears buzzing.

Afterward he always had to go through hours of hating

them all for making him feel ashamed of himself and of the human race. It was with them that he was angry for his having given in to temptation, and the feeling was so strong that it would arouse criminal impulses in him.

With that cow of a Louise too, he'd nearly succumbed to temptation, to a different temptation; and that was a far more serious matter. Until now he'd done only what he'd decided to do, what was necessary, indispensable, as he had written to the newspaper.

All that morning he considered discharging her, but that wouldn't be wise. Was Valentin capable of noticing the difference? Was the redheaded youth, with his nose that was next door to bleeding, able to observe?

The hatter felt weighed down. Previously, even when he'd remained silent and absorbed, he felt a lightness, strange as it may seem. He would show a certain seriousness, but with serenity. He lived all alone, within himself, but giving no sign of any conflict, any apprehension.

If he was less anxious this morning than he'd been the evening before, the trouble he'd felt had entered deeply into him.

He wasn't thinking clearly. The image of that vile Louise pursued him, together with the image of what had almost happened: and then, because of her, others came back to him—images of the district around the barracks, and finally, inevitably, the memory of Madame Binet.

He was busy in his workroom, freshening hats or blocking them. Twice in the course of an hour he had gone into the salesroom to wait on customers, stealing glances at the house across the street.

Suddenly, as he looked at the familiar surroundings—the brown shelves, the mirrors, the wooden heads, the gas stove, his name that he could read in reverse on the window—he had the impression that something there had stopped like a clock.

Nothing of what was around him had changed since he'd first taken over the shop.

Other men had at least tried to move in one direction or another. Even Paul Chantreau, the doctor, had struggled for a long time.

But at twenty-three he himself had come back from Poitiers, where he was studying, to bury himself here, just as certain animals retreat into their burrows at the beginning of winter.

Well, it had been because of Madame Binet. He'd never said so, he'd never admitted it. It wasn't completely true. Yet it was the nearest thing to the truth.

He'd been living in her house, in Poitiers. She was a widow too. He was only beginning to realize how big the population of widows was and how virulent they were.

She was thirty-four or thirty-five. Her husband, while he was still alive, had been a fairly important official, and she owned a fine house in the upper part of the city, where she lived with her son Albert, who at that time was a schoolboy of fourteen.

To augment her income she had decided to rent a room to a student. Monsieur Labbé's mother had heard of it. How? He'd forgotten. It had been arranged through mutual acquaintances, many letters had been exchanged, the two women had met, and Madame Labbé had returned to La Rochelle satisfied that her son was safely provided for.

The first time, it had happened when Léon Labbé had a sore throat. Every year toward fall or at the beginning of winter he would come down with a sore throat. He had not gone to his classes. There were only the two of them in the house. Madame Binet had on a violently blue dressing gown, through the gap of which lace was visible.

He had a slight fever. The room smelled of eucalyptus. She was determined to look after him. She'd

insisted on putting him to bed, and despite her maternal manner they had ended by making love.

It was the first time it had happened to him anywhere except in the district around the barracks. He'd been terrified by his partner's violence, by what took place in her so quickly and left her as if disfigured. Thinking of the boy who was at school and would soon be getting home, he felt guilty.

It had gone on for two and a half years, the two and a half years that he had spent in Poitiers. His friends at the university nicknamed his landlady "the Binette." They claimed that he wasn't the first. Since he was thin in those days, they insisted that she was draining away his entire substance, and it may have been true; she never left him in peace, went to him in his room when her son could hear her, and let herself go as he was never to see another woman do. She was as shameless as possible. She did it on purpose, aggressively; once aroused, she used the foulest words, which he had heard only in brothels and which made him blush.

He didn't dare move to another boardinghouse, for he'd have had to explain the reason to his parents. Then too, she would undoubtedly have followed him wherever he went.

It became a standing joke in class to call him "the Binette's Binet," and during his third year he began feeling that he would fail his examinations. It made him ashamed. When he went home to spend his Easter vacation in La Rochelle, he felt safe in the hat shop in the Rue du Minage, hesitated two or three days longer. The memory of Albert, who was now seventeen, who knew everything and talked to him cynically about his mother, hounded him.

"Since you've always wanted me to come back to the shop," he said to his father one day, "I think I'll decide to do it."

That was all.

It was what he was thinking about today, together with other not much pleasanter things, for he felt a need to take his bearings. He was irresolute. Once or twice he found himself looking into one of the mirrors in the shop, and the sight of his face depressed him. He thought he looked old. He felt curious about the little tailor's health. He pulled the string more often than usual, to have an excuse for going upstairs—so often, indeed, that Valentin summoned up the courage to ask:

"Is Madame Labbé feeling worse?"

He stared at him without answering. Though the sky was as limpid as the mother-of-pearl in an oyster shell, around him there was a fog that distorted the appearance of people and things.

Had that beast of a Louise noticed that the bottle of brandy wasn't in the buffet? He had left it upstairs, and just before noon he went up and took a swallow from it.

He had put off buying the paper at the corner of the street because he knew that it would make him even more depressed.

For the first time, Jeantet wrote solemnly, *the murderer has not done what he announced he would do.*

From this he deduced a whole column of suppositions. Bluff? Illness? Fear of the increase in the police patrols?

Unless the seventh victim, in accordance with the mayor's instructions, did not leave her house.

And Jeantet plunged into the realm of theories.

Was a seventh victim designated? That is what we shall learn in a few days. From the first, the strangler has tried to make us believe that he did not attack just any woman at random, but that he had a definite list, was following a preconceived plan.

Is this true? Is it false? Are we to see in it only an explanation given after the fact, or even a ruse to baffle suspicion or to lend him a certain prestige?

People befoul everything; they can't resist doing it.

Was he going to have to let himself be caught in order to explain the truth, to give him proofs? The idea tempted him, perhaps not very strongly or very sincerely, but it tempted him. Who knows if it wouldn't be the best thing to do?

Kachoudas was still in his armchair, and his wife changed his wet compress every hour. At noon she served him a custard, which he ate slowly with a teaspoon, holding the dish on his lap. Once, hearing the shop bell ring, she went downstairs and talked with a customer, presumably explaining that her husband was ill.

By about two o'clock Monsieur Labbé had already decided to take advantage of the new situation. Everything hung together. Because of the maid, he had thought of the district around the barracks, then of Madame Binet, and he had twice gone back upstairs to drink.

He had a very bad headache. Aspirin did nothing for it. He needed something else. He struggled until four o'clock, the time for turning on the lights, then he put on his overcoat and hat.

"I have an errand to do, Valentin. If I'm not back by six o'clock, you are to shut up the shop."

He had his hand on the doorknob when he turned round and went back into the workroom. His hand reached into the hollow in the wooden head, stayed there for a moment. Terrified, he resisted, for he still had the strength to resist.

He set off again without taking anything and walked toward the Rue Gargoulleau.

He was in the habit of going there occasionally, always at about this time. On the left, a little way before the Place d'Armes, there was an eighteenth-century mansion in which some famous people had lived. The great doorway was still surmounted by a coat of arms and flanked by two stone posts. There was a paved courtyard

with buildings on three sides, and the mansion was now divided into several apartments. There were even some copper name plates at the entrance. The ground floor back was occupied by a dentist whom Monsieur Labbé had known at school. Somewhere else there was a company that sold refrigerators, and the departmental archivist had rooms all the way upstairs.

The left wing was only two stories high and had two entrances. The second door opened directly onto a staircase that led to the second floor, and it was in front of this door that the hatter stopped.

Each time he had come there he'd felt the same little anxiety as he had years ago when he entered the district around the barracks. Yet he wasn't the only one to stop on this threshold. The others, including the doctor, weren't a bit ashamed to tell about it. Chantreau would say bluntly when he arrived late for the card game:

"I stopped by to give Berthe a kiss."

Julien Lambert said nothing, because he was a Protestant, and, especially, because he was terrified of his wife, but he neither denied it nor did much of anything to hide the fact that he went there.

How many of them were there who regularly visited the cozy apartment, all hung with pale satin, with a wealth of carpets, poufs, easy chairs, fragile and charming knickknacks?

Seven or eight. Mademoiselle Berthe was not a common prostitute. For two years she had been kept by Rist, the shipowner—the senior Rist, that is, for there were four or five Rists, who made up a sort of clan in the city, all of them Protestants too, and owners of one of the biggest fortunes in that part of the country.

Rist Senior was sixty at the time. His son and his two daughters were married. One of his sons-in-law was in charge of the company's office in Paris.

The whole family was in the business, and no one ever saw a Rist in a café or in a casino on the coast.

It might be that until he was sixty Rist Senior had never had anything to do with a woman except his wife, who had become so dried up that you could hear her joints crack.

It was he who had rented and furnished Mademoiselle Berthe's apartment. He had been as discreet as possible, yet for two years the entire tribe had nagged at him, including his own children and his sons-in-law.

Rumor had it that there had been epic scenes, that he had even gone down on his knees and begged them to let him enjoy a little pleasure during his last days.

The clan had finally got the upper hand. One evening in the presence of all the Rists he had solemnly sworn never again to set foot in the house in the Rue Gargoulleau and never again to see Mademoiselle Berthe.

Not even to tell her the decision that had just been made. It was one of his sons-in-law who undertook the mission and who had been quite ruthless on the subject of money.

After that Rist Senior had taken the night train to Paris once a month, and rumor had it that he was allowed to go to a high-class brothel near Notre-Dame-de-Lorette.

Mademoiselle Berthe had retained her quiet manner, had continued the cotton-wool existence of a kept woman, but since there was no one in the city who could take the shipowner's place she had opened her door to a few carefully selected customers.

Monsieur Labbé saw light through the slits in the Venetian blinds and knew that she was at home. She was almost always at home but he still had to face the test of the electric bell. Was it she or one of her lovers who had thought of it? In any case, the bell had been equipped with a switch. When she had a visitor she turned it off, and no one persisted, for they all knew what it meant.

Monsieur Labbé reached out, pushed the button, and not a sound came from the other side of the door.

There was somebody there, perhaps the doctor, and

his depression increased. He felt unwell. He needed something, he didn't exactly know what. He had thought he'd find it here, yet he couldn't just wander around the district and come back from time to time and ring again.

He hadn't brought the cello string with him. That didn't necessarily mean that he'd made up his mind. As a matter of fact, he needed the cello string only outdoors, when he had to act very quickly, silently, by surprise.

He hadn't used it for Mathilde, who was in bed.

The truth was that when he had come here he had not made up his mind to anything. Now he walked slowly along the sidewalks, his shoulders sagging. He didn't want to drink any kind of spirits in front of his friends, because it wasn't part of the tradition and he was still being cautious. At least he could go into another café. He'd done that on occasion before. There were several of them near the covered market. He passed in front of the fish stands and recognized one of the fishwives, whom he had desired for at least two years when he was finishing school. He had never spoken to her. In those days she was a street urchin with pointed breasts. He'd more than once seen her in some dark corner with a man. His schoolmates knew her. She was said to do anything she was asked to do and with anyone, and not for money but because she liked it. She'd been given a nickname that vulgarly described one of her accomplishments.

He had never dared, and now she was an old woman sitting on a folding stool behind a display of whitings. Like everyone in the city, she knew who he was. What she couldn't guess was that she had occupied so big a place in his thoughts, or that it was because of her that he'd so often visited the brothels near the barracks, only to find himself nauseated.

He drank two glasses of brandy, and the waiter's eyes

on him made him uncomfortable. Yet the waiter couldn't be thinking of anything.

He had promised himself that he wouldn't go back to the Rue Gargoulleau. He knew the visitor would still be there. Yet he went into the courtyard and pushed the button of the electric bell. No answer.

His hand, in the pocket of his overcoat, mechanically felt for the cello string that wasn't there. Looking somber, almost suspicious, he entered the Café des Colonnes, and he found it unpleasant not to feel the little tailor behind him.

He'd been so calm, so well in control of his nerves, the last few weeks! To be sure, he'd had to think of everything, to calculate his slightest gestures and actions, but he felt confident, he was forging ahead slowly, surely, keeping his list in mind, like a man who has set himself a task and whom thenceforth nothing can turn aside.

The doctor was there. So it wasn't he who was visiting Mademoiselle Berthe today. Nor was it Julien Lambert, who was fiddling with the cards, while the two of them and Arnould waited patiently for a fourth.

Why did Chantreau frown as he saw the hatter sit down? Because it wasn't quite his time yet?

"The usual, Monsieur Labbé?" asked Gabriel, who had a motherly attitude toward all the members of the little group.

"Will you play?"

He would. He had plenty of time to play. He had nothing to do until seven o'clock that evening. From then on he'd have nothing left to do, and that gave him a feeling of a vacuum that was almost dizzying.

He wouldn't even have to take precautions any more!

"You look tired," said Paul Chantreau, studying him over the cards.

"I'm not aware of it."

"It's a strange thing. My colleagues insist that humid-

ity is unhealthy. And every year I observe the same phenomenon here. During the rains, people hold up. But as soon as the first frosts arrive you can't count the cases of grippe and sore throat. I had eleven only this morning.

"Pass."

"Pass."

"One spade."

"Pass."

"Two diamonds."

Monsieur Labbé did not have the flu; he felt sure of that now. The knowledge did not make him any the less ill humored; he was angry with all of them, though he couldn't have said why, just as he was angry with Louise, just as he had been angry with Mademoiselle Berthe for the last hour.

Yet he didn't have a persecution complex. He was not insane. Young Jeantet hadn't succeeded in making an impression on him, either with his arguments or with his newly acquired knowledge of psychiatry.

Jeantet wasn't here, and neither was his employer, Monsieur Caillé. Come to think of it, mightn't it be Caillé, with his big belly and all that hair, who was in bed with Mademoiselle Berthe?

He was angry with him too. He was angry with the little tailor, whose chair remained unoccupied.

It was some time later that Julien Lambert, looking up at the clock and seeing that it was quarter past five, observed:

"Just think of that—you've lost your dog!"

The hatter failed to understand at once. Since he loathed not understanding, he became surly.

"I've never owned a dog," he said gruffly.

The others, who had caught on, burst out laughing.

"Kachoudas isn't in his chair. Usually he gets here right after you. I suspect he sets his watch by yours or waits for you on his doorstep."

Had Julien Lambert something in the back of his mind that made him say such a thing?

"Kachoudas is ill."

"How do you know?"

"I saw him through their window."

"I said three clubs!" Arnould broke in impatiently; he disapproved of talk during a game, for he tended to make mistakes. "Paul passed. Léon passed, I bid three clubs. Your bid, Julien."

It was sticky. Monsieur Labbé couldn't have explained why it was sticky. The weather was dry, the streets flooded with moonlight. The café was not yet filled with tobacco smoke. Oscar, the proprietor, standing there behind them, hadn't yet begun to talk thickly.

It was sticky nevertheless, sticky as birdlime. He must get back to thinking straight again, not let himself give in to confusing sensations.

But it did him good to drink. He'd already emptied his glass, which usually lasted him a half an hour, and had signaled to Gabriel to refill it.

"How is Mathilde?"

One of them was always sure to ask him that. How would they take it if he answered quietly:

"She's been dead for six weeks."

It wasn't often Caillé who asked the question, for he'd been engaged to Mathilde before the hatter. Nobody knew why the engagement had been broken. It had been done discreetly, a year before Monsieur Labbé's marriage. Had they slept together? It was quite possible. In any case, Monsieur Labbé hadn't been the first.

Yet his mother had said to him:

"A remarkably well-brought-up young lady."

And in fact she had been brought up at the Immaculate Conception. Her father was in the customs service, with a fairly high position. Her mother was dead.

"I shan't always be there to look after the house."

Madame Labbé was a diminutive, self-effacing per-

son, who totted up miles a day just hurrying around the rooms. When she passed close to anyone, when there was a customer in the shop, when she made the slightest noise, she would instantly stammer out:

"Excuse me."

He was more like his mother than his father, physically at least. His father was a quiet, strong, self-assured man.

"You know what the doctor said, Léon."

That she didn't have long to live. It had taken ten years during which Madame Labbé Senior hadn't had long to live. A brute of a doctor had unfortunately told her so, and she used it as a kind of blackmail.

"Why don't you marry like everyone else? At your age your father had married."

Was he as glad that he had done so as she implied? In any case he never joined in discussions of this kind, which finally took place almost every day.

They owned a small villa at Fourras, near the pier, where Monsieur Labbé Senior, who loved fishing, had decided to retire someday.

"It's because of you that we don't go to live there right now."

"Then you're making a mistake. I'd manage very well by myself."

It was true. All they need do was leave him the maid, who had been in the house for twenty years.

"Haven't you ever noticed that the little Courtois girl is in love with you?"

The little Courtois girl was Mathilde, whose father often came to the house. She was a brunette, like Madame Binet. In those days she didn't look like the widow he had known in Poitiers, otherwise he'd probably have noticed it. Yet she had the same very dark, very bright eyes, which looked intently at people and things as if to dominate them or assimilate them.

Why had he ended by saying yes? Perhaps because his

mother's health was worse, for now she had several attacks a day. She suffered a great deal, was visibly shriveling up.

"I'd pass on so much more happily if I knew you were married!"

He had become engaged and his mother had died three weeks before the wedding. It had been too late. His father wanted only one thing—to retire at once to his house at Fourras. He had already bought a small boat, which he used on Sundays in summer.

"No trumps?" his partner asked when he had played a six of diamonds.

He looked at his hand, became flustered.

"Excuse me, I have some."

"What were you thinking of?"

"Nothing."

Chantreau looked at him from time to time, covertly but as keenly as if he was determined to diagnose him. Despite his bushy beard and his generally unkempt appearance, he was the most intelligent of them all, and even when he had been drinking—or perhaps especially when he had been drinking—his penetration was frightening.

The hatter hesitated to order a third Picon. He needed it. Right in front of his friends he was undergoing a horrifying adventure. There he was, to all appearances perfectly calm, holding his cards, trying his best to follow the game and managing to make very few mistakes.

And suddenly something broke loose in him: his fingers began to tremble, his sight became blurred, he had the impression that he had grown soft, that his nerves were going back on him, that he was running an immense risk just by remaining seated there in the warmth from the stove, that he must get up at all costs, bestir himself, decide on something and do it.

"Gabriel!"

"Yes, Monsieur Labbé."

Why was Chantreau looking at him? Didn't he have a right to drink three Picons? Did he look drunk?

Perhaps by now there was nobody in the apartment in the Rue Gargoulleau. That recalled a vile memory; he'd made love to a woman near the barracks right after a soldier. No danger of that happening with Mademoiselle Berthe. Of all the women he knew, she would probably have made the pleasantest wife. She was gentle, always smiling. Though she knew men well, she had an instinctive respect for them which in her case amounted to a sort of discreet indulgence. Her character was like her complexion, like the curves of her body, the consistency of her flesh, like the setting she had created for herself.

Very soon now he would be back with Louise in the badly lit dining room, where the electric light had always been yellowish. He would have to resist, for it was taking hold of him again. He wanted to have it over and done with.

It was vague. It didn't mean anything. The problem was to find out if drinking was doing him good or, on the contrary, was making him feel dizzier.

He could have asked Chantreau. He almost wanted to. What prevented him from waiting until Paul left—it wouldn't delay him much—and then going out with him as if by chance?

"Just a minute, Paul!"

He had a perfect right to insist on professional secrecy. So it was even less dangerous than with Kachoudas.

"I want your advice about something. I killed Mathilde one night."

Calmly. Above all, he must explain to him that he'd done it calmly, deliberately. As it happened, he'd just come from the auction room, where he'd bought the odd volumes of the nineteenth-century trials. He'd begun

with Madame Lafarge's, whose story he knew only vaguely.

At least every quarter of an hour, when he was sitting by the fire, he would hear a hard, venomous voice calling him:

"Léon!"

There was no use pretending not to hear it. The tone was unanswerable. She'd adopted it long ago, long before her illness, almost immediately after they were married, at just about the same time that she'd begun to look like Madame Binet. For one day he'd discovered the resemblance, which had never struck him before. It was the same voice, the same assurance; above all, it was the same possessive manner.

He would hardly have begun a chapter before, not even looking up and scarcely moving her lips, she would bring out:

"Léon!"

And he'd have to get up. She would take her time about telling him what she wanted, sometimes a glass of water, sometimes that he should pull up or turn down the bedclothes, or bring her a chamberpot, or give her one of her pills. She was too hot or too cold, or the light hurt her eyes.

It was all lies. She made it all up, spent her time, from the moment he sat down again, making up something else.

She watched him coldly while he obeyed her orders, and she never said thank you.

She had long been suspicious of him, ever since the fourth or fifth year of her illness, when she began to insist that he meant to free himself by poisoning her.

That wasn't true, either. She didn't really believe it. It was another invention to torment him.

"You've eaten onions again, on purpose to make me sick with your breath. Don't be so impatient. I shan't last much longer."

He seldom managed to read two pages without being interrupted. He had to begin the same passage over again two or three times, wound up by confusing the names and dates.

"Léon!"

She knew that this particular book interested him deeply, and she had racked her brains for new excuses ever since he'd begun it.

"Read me some of it aloud."

He loathed doing that. Especially because then she would ask him to explain the previous chapters, didn't understand, made him go back.

"Léon!"

She wasn't thirsty. She didn't need a chamberpot. She pretended, with a little gleam of treachery lighting up her eyes. He was her property! It was all she still owned in the world, but she really owned him and she needed to assure herself of it constantly. That was why she refused to have either a nurse or a servant enter her room, why she refused to see anyone at all. That way she owned him more surely. He had no excuse for going, even for a moment, to breathe any other air than that which surrounded her.

"Léon!"

In fifteen years he hadn't read a single book in peace, yet it was his last refuge.

He had got only halfway through the story of Madame Lafarge, just to the testimony of the pharmacist who had sold the poison.

"Léon!"

The narrative was all gray, without a ray of sunlight. The whole thing took place inside stifling walls, and you couldn't imagine any of the characters smiling even once, the way everybody does.

"Léon!"

So one evening he had got up for the last time and shut his book. Had she understood that there'd been a

change in him? Had she sensed that he had at last come to a decision?

"As you see, Paul, I was very calm, terribly calm. I'd known for a long time that it was bound to happen."

How would the doctor have reacted?

The hatter had just made a little slam, mechanically, from force of habit. Chantreau was looking at him keenly again.

No! He wouldn't understand at all. It would be making a useless effort. Besides, his case had nothing to do with medicine. He wasn't ill. He wasn't insane. There was nothing wrong with him.

"Gabriel!"

Why not? He was thinking less about Louise, who reminded him of a big country feather bed. He saw her huge, as when you have a fever and feel your fingers, your hand, your whole body swell, when it seems as if you filled the whole room.

He laughed sardonically, for young Jeantet was back in his place. He hadn't seen him come in. There he was, solemnly blackening a sheet of paper on the marble table.

He must think he was really somebody!

It was on that evening—Tuesday, December 14—that
he began to write. He hadn't waited for Chantreau
before he left the Café des Colonnes. He remembered
thinking, as he opened the door:

"Now that my back's turned, what are they going to
say?"

There was one thing he knew that he didn't like. He
had never referred to it. Besides, it was really very
unimportant. When they talked about him in his
absence—he'd heard them once when they hadn't
known he was there—they didn't say either "Labbé" or
"Léon," but "the hatter."

It wasn't even worth thinking about, of course. They
could have answered him that they also said "the doctor," "the senator"; but that was different; those
sounded like titles of honor. The proof was that it didn't
occur to anyone to say "the insurance agent" or "the
printer."

It had been at least ten years ago that he'd happened
to make this trivial discovery; he'd mentioned it to no
one, and he hadn't held it against them—which showed
that it didn't affect him.

The Rue du Minage was horribly empty—not a
sound, not a footstep ahead of him or behind him. The
unshaded light in the little tailor's window had something dreary about it.

He did what he had to do, but for the first time he did
it as if he were above doing it, with supreme contempt,
speaking the words without believing in them, as some
people go on saying their prayers.

"Has Madame called?"

She didn't need to feel afraid, the filthy slut—he would never touch her. He was sure of himself now. Whatever happened, it wouldn't be her he'd attack.

He went upstairs, forced himself to say something. He forgot none of the ritual. He moved the armchair, went and looked out the window, and received a shock when, in the workroom across the street, he saw Madame Kachoudas talking with Dr. Martens. Kachoudas was not in the room. He must have been put to bed. For those people to send for a doctor, the case must be really serious. He remembered the birth of their youngest child, four years earlier. The midwife hadn't arrived until it was all over.

It was clear that she was speaking in a low voice, that she was asking questions, and that Martens—who belonged to the generation between forty and fifty— was having trouble answering.

Was Kachoudas going to die? The thought terrified Monsieur Labbé, and to such a degree that he very nearly went downstairs to wait for the doctor in the street and question him too.

When Martens had gone, Esther was sent to the pharmacy again, this time with a prescription, and he saw the girl hesitate, realized at once that she was afraid of the strangler. It was ridiculous. He would have liked to call out to her that she was in no danger.

He ate dinner. He took the tray upstairs. He threw Mathilde's meal into the toilet bowl and pulled the chain several times. There was something he couldn't get off his mind. Through it all his face wore the expression of a man who has an overwhelming task, an immense responsibility.

Could Louise have noticed that he smelled of drink? Hadn't she admitted to him that her father got drunk every Sunday and that they usually had to carry him to

his bed and lay him on it fully dressed, only taking off his shoes?

He mustn't forget anything. He forgot nothing. He went down to the cellar and brought up another bottle of brandy, had to pass less than six feet from Mathilde, but didn't even think of it. More precisely, he thought of it as he went up again, on the stairs. He observed that it aroused no emotion in him to go down into the cellar and to remember what had happened on November 2, the day after All Saints' Day.

If he had been following his ritual scrupulously, once the logs were in the fireplace and he had put on his dressing gown, he would have begun by cutting out the printed letters he would need to answer the article in the newspaper. But it was so useless! He could convey almost nothing that way!

He walked round and round like a dog trying to decide where to lie down, smoked almost a whole pipe without making up his mind, went and looked out the window once again, and saw, sitting beside the tailor's table, the two women, Madame Kachoudas and Esther, talking together in whispers and now and again looking anxiously toward the door at the back of the room.

Then he suddenly sat down at the little desk, opened the drawer, and took out a sheet of letter paper, business paper with the letterhead of his shop, which showed that from now on he was beyond caring about precautions. He poured himself a glass of brandy and took a sip of it before he began.

It is of no consequence what will be thought and said . . .

That wasn't true, since he was going to the trouble of writing. It wasn't entirely false, either. His message wasn't intended for everyone indiscriminately. But, for one example, he wouldn't have wanted the little tailor to leave this world without knowing.

It was extremely complicated, and his head hurt.

He'd had a headache all day. He was taken aback at the sight of his handwriting. It was because of what he'd drunk, presumably, because of his fingers being shaky. The letters were not the same size, and some of them overlapped.

It was very hot in the bedroom, as always. Yet he felt something like a chill breath on his left cheek, for it was three feet from the window and the panes were frosted over.

What he ought to make clear was that, until now, he had acted lucidly, knowing exactly all that was involved. He thought he'd found the right expression:

I have assumed, and I continue to assume, all my responsibilities.

That wasn't quite so, either. He had assumed them—yes. But was he sure of assuming them in the future? Wasn't that just what terrified him?

Say what they would, all through his life he had accepted his responsibilities, calmly. It was not really true that he'd become a hatter because of that "Binette," whom he hated almost as much as he did Louise.

He'd make that clear. No—that would be going back too far. He'd never be finished. It concerned only a few people. He understood himself. It was perfectly clear in his own mind.

What had happened, for example, in the case of the girls in the photograph, of the fifteen classmates who had left the convent of the Immaculate Conception the same year? Some of them had gone away, others had stayed. Some of them had got married, and some had remained single.

One of them, of her own accord, of her own free will, without any pressure from outside, had simply given up. It was the one who was still in the convent under the name of Mother Sainte-Ursule.

Very well! The same phenomenon occurred in the case of men, was repeated in every generation. It was a

pity he didn't have a photograph of the group of men who were now in their sixties.

On the one hand: the Chantreaus, the Caillés, the Julien Lamberts, Laude the senator, Lucien Arnould, and a few others who seldom or never showed up at the Café des Colonnes but who had remained faithful to the city.

On the other hand: those who had left to take their chances in Bordeaux, in Paris, or elsewhere. Among them there was even one who was well known to have become a very high administrative official in Indochina.

There were some who reappeared from time to time—for a wedding or a funeral, or to see their families who had remained in the vicinity. They usually dropped in at the Colonnes. And they seemed bent on surrounding themselves with an aura of superiority. Their manner was at once familiar and slightly distant—in short, condescending.

"Well, how's our dear old city getting on?"

Especially the ones who had succeeded, news of whom occasionally appeared in the papers.

"You lead the good life here," they would sigh, at the same time making it clear that they didn't believe a word of it.

Among this latter sort was an advocate who had become a celebrated criminal lawyer and who was talked of as likely to become president of the bar.

Monsieur Labbé had been given a choice too, and he had chosen the hat shop in the Rue du Minage.

Incidentally, some people supposed it was the house in which he had been born. That was not so. To be sure, he had been born in the Rue du Minage, and in a house exactly like the one in which he now lived, but it was fifty yards farther down the street, and he had been eight years old when his parents had moved.

Madame Binet had nauseated him, just as, forty years

later, Louise nauseated him. Yet he could have stayed on in Poitiers in spite of her, or even have gone to Paris.

He had chosen La Rochelle. Not from fear of the struggle. He wasn't afraid, he wasn't afraid of anything.

Who had it been who'd chosen to do his military service in the dragoons, when he'd never touched a horse all through his boyhood? It was he. He'd even enlisted before he was called up, so that he could have a choice of services.

And during the 1914 war, who had asked to be transferred to the air force?

He again—Léon Labbé. After a series of mysterious transfers, when the war broke out he'd been assigned to an infantry regiment. He'd experienced the trenches. He had suffered there, in the mud, in the mob, in the nameless mass that was shifted about like so much matter.

Once he'd become an aviator, he'd never been afraid. At the very most, he would condescend to drug himself with a glass of spirits when, alone in his fighter plane, he would take off on a mission.

He lived in a world apart, among an elite. An orderly took care of him, of his clothes, of his laced boots.

He hadn't even been wounded. They had been the two most congenial years of his life.

But he'd never be finished if he went back that far, although he had a confused feeling that it was indispensable to his record.

I have always chosen deliberately, and I continue and will continue to choose, he wrote on the paper with the letterhead of the hat shop, at the same time listening to Louise coming upstairs to bed.

What he had done could not be called abandoning the struggle, or retreating, or giving up.

It was he, on the contrary, who as the years went by would smile more and more pityingly when he saw the

men from Paris come back to their birthplace for a few
days and think they had to show off. He knew very well
that he had been right, that he had taken the proper
course.

Later, I chose to marry.

That was almost true too, for a house needs a woman
in it, and it's disgusting to go out every now and again to
satisfy oneself somewhere or anywhere. At that period
there wasn't yet a Mademoiselle Berthe in the Rue
Gargoulleau. You had to sink very low, into filth.

He hadn't chosen Mathilde. That wasn't quite true,
either. He'd chosen not to quarrel with his mother,
chosen to please her because she was ill, because he
thought the difference between one respectable girl and
another wasn't worth wasting his time over and hurting
someone else.

After founding the Civilian Aviation Club—for it was
he who had founded it—he had, again, chosen to resign
from it because the shipowner Borin had been named
president of it, though with proper apologies to himself,
for Borin, who was rich and proud, was likely to con-
tribute generously to the club treasury.

He could have been secretary, vice-president. He
had preferred to be nothing.

It was not out of pique or from a want of fighting
spirit. If he'd taken the trouble to oppose Borin's candi-
dacy, he would have won. It was he and he alone who
had considered that it wasn't worth the trouble.

This feeling, which was so clear in his own mind and
heart, was almost impossible to express. For his part, he
felt something in his life like a continuous line, which he
could have drawn with his pen. But words confused
everything, said too much or too little.

And that slut of a Louise was beginning her loathsome
daily racket in her room. She made as much noise all by
herself in a space eight yards square as a whole barrack-
ful of soldiers. He heard her shoes drop on the floor one

after the other; he guessed she was pulling her dress up over her head, panting, her face coming out of it all red; he even thought he saw her rub her breasts as soon as they were freed from the bra, and then the red line that the elastic in her underdrawers left around her waist.

It had been by his own choice again that he hadn't slept with her. He could have done it. Who knows if it wasn't what she'd always expected? She would have lain down unprotestingly. Maybe she couldn't understand why he didn't come to take her?

Had he realized that he'd been very near to doing it in the beginning, and that he was still angry with himself for having been tempted?

They called him "the hatter," as if it were an insult, or at least a funny word, a joke.

But he'd chosen to finish off Mathilde, and her dead body had left him unmoved, he had felt no remorse. Not for a moment, when he was tightening his grip and she had looked at him more in amazement than in terror, had he softened.

Perhaps it had really been decided much too long before, without his knowing it. He'd said to himself:

"If she goes too far . . ."

He had set that "too far" very far away indeed, so as to give her a chance. He had borne it patiently for fifteen years. He had let out so much line that she'd supposed she could get away with anything.

He hadn't got rid of her because of Madame Lafarge, but because she had overdone it.

Louise, who was new to the house then, still slept in a room that he had rented for her in the city, an attic in the Place du Marché, above a textile shop.

Afterward he had had the whole night ahead of him and he had taken his time, so as not to leave anything to chance.

The cellar floor was not cemented. A good third of its surface, under the ventilator, was covered with coal.

He'd worked hard cleaning part of this space and digging almost three feet into the ground. He'd carried Mathilde's body down on his back, which wasn't easy on the spiral staircase, then he'd gone up again to get a sheet from the bedroom for modesty's sake.

He hadn't even forgotten to block up the ventilator while he was at work, for people might have been surprised to see light in the cellar all night long.

At five o'clock in the morning it was all finished; the coal was back in its place, the ventilator uncovered. He'd washed the steps of the staircase one by one, then cleaned up his clothes in the bathtub.

At that point he'd supposed that his task was done. He'd decided on the precautions he must take—which had been easy, since Mathilde refused to see anyone and, for years now, he'd been the only human being to enter her room.

There are those who will claim that I wanted to free myself. That is nonsense.

He knew, before he acted, that he would be very little freer than before, since he'd have to behave as if his wife were still alive and so would have to go through the same set of actions every day, stay at home during the same hours.

She had gone too far—that was all there was to it.

The first day he had been almost gay. It was amusing to take the meals upstairs and throw the food into the toilet, to keep on not eating fish because Mathilde couldn't stand the smell of it, to pull the string to imitate the sound of her cane on the floor, to push the wooden head in front of the window, to talk aloud to himself as he walked up and down the room.

"Has Madame called?"

Valentin hadn't suspected anything. Neither had Louise. At least she'd shown no sign of doing so.

It was on the fifth day that he'd been brought up stock still in front of the group photograph, which was still

hanging on the wall. Then, for just a moment, his self-possession had deserted him, he had turned pale, he had felt really afraid.

For it was not entirely true that no one entered her room. Ever since she'd been bedridden, there had been a tradition: each year on her birthday, December 24, as many of her old schoolmates as still lived in the city would come to bring her their good wishes and their presents.

By now they were all old women or old maids, yet on that day they chattered like schoolgirls.

He had had to face the situation coolly. He could go to call on them one after the other a few days before Christmas, tell them that Mathilde wasn't feeling well and preferred not to see anyone.

He'd have to do it all over again the next year, and then the years after that, until they were all dead; and after a while it might begin to look suspicious.

He had six weeks before him. He knew the history and the habits of each of them. It was almost all that Mathilde ever talked about. When she felt well she told him endless stories of her days at the convent, as excitedly as if it had been only yesterday. She would still sometimes dream of Mother Sainte-Josephine, after more than forty years.

"Last night I dreamed that Anne-Marie Lange told me . . ."

She often jumped from the past to the present without any transition.

"I wonder if Rosalie Cujas is happy. At this time of day she must be in her shop in the Rue des Merciers."

He had thought a great deal. What had struck him most, when Mathilde died, was the speed with which it had been accomplished.

The others were in good health, of course, but they were all more or less the same age. It had taken him several days to think of the cello string, which he'd

climbed up to the third floor to get, going by way of the blind alley.

He had chosen. He hadn't supinely taken the easiest way. He had faced all the possibilities, and what he'd decided on was not particularly agreeable.

I swear that I have felt no perverted pleasure, he wrote toward half past ten in the evening.

He was not drunk. He was convinced that alcohol had nothing to do with what he was feeling. The proof was that he'd felt it ever since that morning, and even the evening before, on the Quai Duperré, when the little tailor was at his heels.

A comparison came into his mind. He wrote it down, for he thought it would be useful, from now on, to record everything. He knew that by the following morning it might not be so clear in his memory.

And clarity was now the most important thing of all. As a boy, he'd had very good eyesight. So for him, images had been perfectly clear, everything stood out precisely, the outlines of objects, their colors, the smallest details.

At that time his grandmother—his father's mother— was still alive, and she wore silver-rimmed spectacles. The lenses were thick, like magnifying glasses, and he sometimes amused himself by putting them in front of his eyes, and things immediately became blurred, their proportions changed, he discovered the world as if through a drop of water.

Until the incident at the bishop's palace—properly speaking, the lack of incident, for nothing had happened—everything had been perfectly clear, and even clearer than in the past, with staring colors, contrasting blacks and whites, lines as if drawn with ink.

He had been going straight ahead, doing what he'd decided to do, had no need to drink to bolster his self-possession, and the word itself didn't enter his mind.

When he got home he would mentally cross out a

name on the list, a face in the photograph, enjoying the satisfaction of having performed his task.

So he had now reached the point of considering this period one of the happiest and fullest in his life, perhaps equal to his time in the air force, when, in those days too, he would calmly count the number of enemy planes he'd shot down, the palms on his Croix de Guerre.

As in the air force, he was constantly up against danger. He had to think of everything, have reflexes he could count on, leave nothing to chance.

As he'd done during the war too, he said to himself: "In a few weeks it will be all over and I'll have no worries."

He didn't have nightmares, didn't feel troubled. He'd got used to an odd little fever that came over him just as he set out on one of his expeditions, to the feeling of relief that he felt when he got home afterward.

Would it still be like that if Mother Sainte-Ursule had gone out on Monday, as she ought to have done, and he'd got all the way through his list?

He wrote on, with jerky movements of his hand that he couldn't control:

Nothing has changed, since her death is really unnecessary. She never entered the house. On the 24th of this month she will do no more than she has done all the other years—she will send her best wishes and a religious picture. And it has always been I who have written to thank her, in Mathilde's name.

In any case, I have nothing against her. I have nothing to gain from her death.

It follows that my task is finished. I have accomplished exactly what I set myself to do.

It wasn't true, and it was at this point that he became perturbed, began a sort of frantic search into the most remote corners of his existence, so uneasy that he seemed ready to jump out of his skin.

Now he simply had to drink in order to keep his

self-possession, in order not to feel his nerves give way again, in order to avoid the inner panic that had nothing to do with fear.

For he wasn't afraid, not of anything, not even of being arrested. On the contrary, that would give him an excellent opportunity to explain. They would have to listen to him, and he would take all the time he needed.

There had been times when he'd wanted to do something risky on purpose, to brush against danger as he'd done in his airplane when he'd skimmed close over the enemy trenches despite the regulations.

What he had to emphasize, what was important, more important than anything else on earth, was that he had never stopped being lucid.

Then why, all of a sudden, for no reason, had the mechanism gone wrong? He wasn't deluding himself. He could have taken it for the beginning of a bad cold, but that wasn't so. Valentin had a cold, Kachoudas was ill. Not he.

Yet around him and inside him the world was beginning to look like what he'd seen long ago through his grandmother's spectacles.

He had not gone to Mademoiselle Berthe's in his usual frame of mind. He was frank with himself: when he set out he hadn't felt the slightest desire to make love.

Nor had he decided to do anything else, and he hadn't brought the cello string with him.

That was precisely what was so serious. It was the same in Louise's case. He'd done nothing to Louise, he was convinced that he would do nothing to her, yet the temptation still persisted, not in his mind, which despised the fat stupid wench, but in some secret place in his flesh.

Jeantet had been cruel when he'd quoted that remark of the psychiatrist in Lyon:

He will not stop till he gets caught.

Why? The fellow had never seen him, knew nothing about him, and he took it on himself, at that distance, as if from some unscalable height, to determine his destiny with fiendish assurance.

He got up and went to look out the window, and there was still a light on across the street. Madame Kachoudas was alone, dozing in the wicker armchair. The alarm clock stood on the tailor's table.

So it was serious. Or else there was some medicine that had to be given at regular intervals. Probably pneumonia. Monsieur Labbé felt certain that the little tailor had refused to let himself be taken to the hospital.

That sort of people stick to their homes, are born and die at home.

Why did the idea of his neighbor's possibly dying throw him into a panic? Kachoudas was of no use to him. They scarcely knew each other. And now all of a sudden he seemed to be clinging to him.

Something had gone wrong. Everything had gone wrong. Three times already this evening he'd sworn it was the last glass he'd drink before he went to bed, and each time he'd poured himself another.

He had let the fire go out, had filled two pages with writing the sight of which made him uneasy.

When had he begun writing so badly, with missing letters and letters that overlapped? He'd heard of graphology. It had been discussed at the Colonnes. He remembered that Paul Chantreau had said:

"Claims have been pressed too far, but at bottom there's a certain amount of scientific truth in it. The people who say they can discover the past and the future in handwriting are either fakers or dupes. Yet it remains true that a person's character can be read in it and, very often, his state of health. A patient with heart trouble, for example, won't write like one with tuberculosis. . . ."

It didn't really matter what he'd said. Monsieur

Labbé had never been ill except for his annual bouts of sore throat; he didn't have heart trouble. He'd been thoroughly examined only six months before.

He wouldn't drink any more; it was dangerous, it put his nerves on edge. Back at the café, Chantreau had already looked at him in a peculiar way.

Since his task was accomplished, he wouldn't even read the newspapers. Jeantet could go on reasoning about his case. As for the other reporters, the fact that nothing more was happening would eventually make them lose interest. For there had been reporters who had come from Paris, six or seven of them at first; they had put up at the Hôtel des Étrangers and had chosen the Café de la Poste, opposite the town hall, as their headquarters.

As the thing dragged on and on, some of them had gone back to Paris, but there must still be at least three of them, including a photographer who could be seen in the streets with his camera on his stomach and a huge pipe in his mouth.

There were also the correspondents for a newspaper in Bordeaux and for another in Nantes, but they both lived in the city and spent the greater part of their time in a bar near the clock tower. They both knew Monsieur Labbé, and greeted him by name.

All he need do was to hold out. Everything he'd written this evening was stupid. It didn't explain anything. He hadn't found the right words. He thought he'd made things clear by underlining certain passages, but it made sense only to him.

He'd start over again, begin right at the beginning, calmly, collectedly. What he wrote would probably never be read. That didn't matter at all. They were things he needed to say, if only to himself.

The fire had only just gone out, but the room was already getting cold, and the hatter was scarcely aware that he was walking back and forth with his hands in his

pockets, that the hands of the alarm clock were moving round, and that he had long ago let his usual time go by.

Was he calm enough?

He drank another mouthful, felt better. He was becoming more and more certain that everything would come out right. The little tailor would get well. Someday, perhaps, he'd talk to him, perfectly simply.

To reassure him, to put him at ease again, he would say:

"It's all over, you know, Kachoudas. No use thinking about it any longer."

It was odd, but it seemed to him it was his own fault that the little tailor was ill, and he felt remorse for it. He would have liked to find out how he was getting on. What could stop him from going to inquire the next day? They were neighbors, greeted each other across the street every morning. When she heard the bell on the shop door ring, Madame Kachoudas would come downstairs.

Afterward she would go and tell her husband:

"The hatter has come to ask after you."

Kachoudas would be frightened. God knows what he'd imagine. It was impossible. He mustn't do it.

He mustn't do anything more, except stick to his schedule, to the acts he had set himself to perform. Follow his schedule exactly—that was the thing!

He listened. As it happened, he had just put his hand on the bottle. It was the last swallow. Tomorrow he'd throw the rest of his stock of brandy into the refuse bin and would drink only his two daily Picons during the bridge game.

Someone was walking in the house. It was an unfamiliar sound. Something rustled against the door.

An ugly voice said:

"Can't you let people get any sleep? What's the matter with you? What do you mean walking around all night like an idiot?"

For a moment he stood there motionless, absolutely motionless. He wasn't far from the door. He had only to put out his hand in order to turn the key in the lock.

"I mustn't do it, no matter what!"

He did it. He opened the door wide, and he saw, exactly in the center of the doorway, like a poorly lighted picture, Louise in a white cotton-flannel nightgown, with her hair down, and barefoot—it was because she was barefoot that her steps hadn't made the same sound as usual.

He was still holding the bottle, and it was at the bottle that she first stared with a look of astonishment, then at the hatter's face. She didn't understand. She didn't yet feel fear. With her make-up off, she had oddly pale lips. Her breasts, under the nightgown, were as swollen as udders.

He did not stir. He remained deliberately motionless, and perhaps did not even breathe during all that time.

She saw the room behind him, and her eyes moved over the two empty beds, stopped on the armchair, the wooden head.

Then she opened her mouth wide for a scream that never came. She must have wanted to run at the top of her speed. He felt it. But she couldn't move either.

It was he who first struggled out of his immobility. The brandy bottle smashed on the floor.

Instead of resisting, Louise fell limply, and he fell on top of her, with his head on the landing and one foot caught between two of the staircase balusters.

She was still warm and damp; her armpits gave off a strong smell. One of her hands seized the hatter's ear; it seemed as if she was trying to tear it off.

When he got up he staggered. He had just strength enough left to go back into the room and, without shutting the door, to let himself fall on the edge of Mathilde's bed.

He didn't look at the clock. He never knew how long it

had taken. He had had the feeling that he was tumbling down into an abyss, as in a nightmare, and he lay there staring at the rug, not daring to raise his head.

His first definite sensation was of a gentle warmth: the blood that flowed from his lacerated ear was running down his neck and tickling him.

He moved his head a little and saw Louise's bare feet and legs, her bare abdomen, her torn nightgown.

The brandy bottle was broken to bits. With his body drained, he got up, rushed to the bathroom to drink a glass of water, and had just time to lean over the washbasin to vomit.

8

That morning again he couldn't call out across the street:

"Good morning, Kachoudas."

The tailor certainly wasn't getting better. If the little girls had left for school, Esther, the eldest, didn't seem inclined to go to her shop. At half past eight she hadn't begun dressing, and now she was cleaning the house, while her mother probably slept.

It was the day for the street peddlers' market. There was a roar in the direction of the covered market, and in the Rue du Minage there were a few old women, always the same ones in the same places, with a folding stool and a few baskets of vegetables or chestnuts or live poultry.

When Valentin arrived, Monsieur Labbé was just finishing sweeping the shop and pushing the dust out into the street through the open door. The clerk didn't notice anything unusual. His employer said to him in his deep voice—he had a fine voice:

"Good morning, Valentin. How do you feel?"

And he looked at him with interest.

"I think it's getting better, sir," the young man answered, sniffling. "I'm coughing a little this morning, but my mother says it's because it's leaving by way of my throat."

Everything appeared to be in order in the house. The gas stove was burning. Monsieur Labbé was calm, rather kindly, which was the case now and again. On those days he had a fatherly attitude toward Valentin, spoke in a more unctuous voice, and sometimes even did his best to make him laugh.

He was freshly shaved, as always, had on a clean shirt, his shoes were polished and his necktie neatly knotted.

"I feel rather uneasy, Valentin. Yesterday evening, when I was with Madame Labbé, I heard Louise go out. I thought she was going to meet some boy friend at the corner of the street, and I waited to fasten the bolt. But she hasn't come back."

"Do you think she was strangled?"

"In any case, I shall notify the police."

Once again he was doing what he had to do. Contrary to what he had expected, his face wasn't swollen or his eyes unsteady, as they had been the night before. His hands weren't shaking. He was calm and serious, without any of the uneasiness that usually follows on broken sleep.

For he had slept. When he'd come out of the bathroom he'd sat down in the armchair by the burnt-out fire, and never in all his life had he felt so empty. Hadn't he literally just emptied himself in every possible way?

He had looked at nothing, thought of nothing, and less than five minutes later, he sank into a deep, dreamless sleep. When he'd opened his eyes, the hands of the alarm clock on the mantelpiece pointed to the same hour as they did when he got up on other days, and he himself was already in the state he was in now, calm, very calm, moving a trifle slowly, with an extreme inward tiredness, but also an immense relief.

His mind went into gear perfectly naturally. He needed to reflect, to see where things stood, but he took nothing tragically.

It was too late to carry the body down the cellar, and in any case he didn't feel that he had energy enough to move the pile of coal today. He pulled Louise into the bedroom by her feet and shoved her under Mathilde's bed. There was no use hiding her. If anyone went into the room, everything would inevitably be discovered. It wasn't the maid that mattered. It was Mathilde.

However, he preferred not to see the fat slut every time he had to go upstairs.

He lit the fire and, as on other mornings, did all that he had to do; he also made coffee. He even found that he was speaking as he came and went in the room, whereas today there was no need of it.

There was still a light on across the street. Madame Kachoudas, who had not gone to bed that night, was languidly cooking breakfast.

What troubled him the most was going into the maid's room, but it had to be done. The bed was unmade, with stains on the sheets. He had to make it. The comb was full of hairs. The smell nauseated him. Underwear and dresses were scattered helter-skelter; there were two cheap suitcases in a corner.

It was better not to pretend that she'd left with her belongings. It would be enough to remove the clothes she'd worn the day before, provided he didn't forget anything: stockings, shoes, panties, bra, petticoat, dress. Her coat too, for with the weather as cold as it was, she wouldn't have gone out without a coat.

He came very near to ruining everything. He was just about to go downstairs when, by a miracle, he thought of her hairpins, and they turned out to be what he most shrank from touching. He threw them into the toilet bowl, as he had done Mathilde's food on other days. As for the clothes, he'd let it go at stuffing them under the bed with the body.

Had he forgotten anything? He went back to Louise's room, opened the drawer in the bedside table, saw a box encrusted with sea shells. It contained some rings and bracelets, of the kind sold at fairs, two or three picture postcards, a key, no doubt to one of the suitcases, some small change, and the picture of a young man with thick, unruly hair, a peasant in his Sunday best who'd posed for his photograph in a painted cardboard airplane. He left it there.

That was all. Everything else was a chance he had to take, and he felt confident. What most preoccupied him was Kachoudas' illness. Twice he found Madame Kachoudas looking over toward the hat shop from the windows across the street.

Had the little tailor told her anything? Had he merely asked her:

"What is Monsieur Labbé doing?"

Might he be delirious? And if he was seriously ill, wouldn't he send for a priest?

He felt an urge to go and see him. It was next to impossible. Doing so just wouldn't fit in with their acknowledged relationship.

Yet the idea remained in the back of his mind.

"I'll probably be back in half an hour, Valentin. I don't think my wife will call."

"Yes, sir."

He put on his overcoat, his hat, came very near to destroying the cello string. He also thought of the string in the closet that gave the signal on the second floor. What was the use? No matter what, if the house was searched, the truth would come out.

The sun was already almost warm, the city looked really gay that morning. He hadn't had a drink. He'd taken great care not to drink. Indeed, he scarcely even wanted to.

He crossed the Place d'Armes diagonally, took the Rue Réaumur, came to the building where Pigeac had his office. It was not really an administrative building, but a very big and handsome private house that had recently been made over into offices. The ground floor was occupied by the national insurance office, where most of the employees were girls

He went up to the second floor. A door stood open. Three men were moving about in a thick cloud of smoke. The stove wasn't working properly, belched all the smoke out into the room, so that the windows that gave

onto the courtyard had had to be opened. Pigeac, with his overcoat and hat on, waited, sitting on the edge of his desk.

"Well, well!" he said. "The hatter!"

"Good morning, Monsieur Pigeac."

A second open door gave onto a bathroom, in which the tub had been left, though shelves had been put up and were full of files.

Monsieur Labbé coughed because of the smoke. Pigeac was coughing too, and his two detectives were trying to deal with the stove.

"You must excuse me for receiving you like this; it's been two weeks since I asked for the chimney to be cleaned, and nothing has come of it. Would you rather we went out on the landing?"

It wasn't very impressive—almost the opposite.

"What good wind brings you, Monsieur Labbé?"

"I am afraid, Inspector, that it is an ill wind. To tell you the truth, I really know nothing. Possibly I am being alarmed for no reason."

He was sure enough of himself to make a point of speaking with elaborate precision.

"I imagine I am not the first person to trouble you since the recent events. Like everyone else, I have a maid, a country girl—from Charron, to be exact. You are doubtless aware of my wife's state of health; for years she has refused to see anyone and lives confined to her room. That is why our maid slept out until recently, in a room I rented for her in the Place du Marché."

Pigeac listened, looking at him attentively, even with a certain keenness, but that was the way he looked at everybody, thinking that it gave him an added importance. The shrill chatter of the girls working downstairs in the national insurance office was plainly audible.

It all seemed rather the reverse of serious.

"After the murders began to terrorize our towns-

people, Louise asked me for permission to sleep in the house so that she would not have to go out after nightfall. Despite my wife's reluctance, I had to accept, otherwise she would have left us."

"How long has she been sleeping in your house?"

"About three weeks. If I remember rightly, it began immediately after the death of Madame Cujas."

"Does she sleep on the same floor as you and your wife?"

"Yes, on the second floor, in a small room that looks out on the courtyard. Yesterday evening about nine o'clock—I cannot be quite sure of the time, since I was busy taking care of my wife—I heard her going downstairs. I thought she had forgotten something in the kitchen or wanted to make herself a hot drink."

"Did she do that sometimes?"

"No. And that was why I eventually became uneasy. I went downstairs myself. I did not find her. I saw that the bolt on the shop door had been opened, and that was how I knew she had gone out, for I had fastened the bolt myself before I went upstairs."

"And she didn't come back?"

"No. Not last night, and not this morning. I waited up quite late for her. This morning I found her room just as it was yesterday. The bed had not been slept in."

"Did she take her things with her?"

"I think not. I saw two suitcases, and some dresses in the closet."

"Is she a well-behaved girl?"

"I have never had occasion to complain of her behavior."

"Is it the first time she's gone out at night?"

"Since she has been living in my house, yes."

"I'll go with you."

Pigeac went into the office, which was still gray with smoke, and spoke briefly to his detectives. Then he

showed Monsieur Labbé down the stairs. He was polite but cold. In the street, he made the hatter walk on his right, perhaps unintentionally.

"Do you know her family?"

"I only know that her parents have a small farm in Charron. She went to see them every Sunday, leaving in the morning and returning in the evening."

"At what time?"

"By the bus that arrives at the Place d'Armes at nine o'clock. I always heard her come in about five minutes after nine."

They passed the Café des Colonnes, where Gabriel, who was cleaning the windows, greeted them.

They had fallen into step together. It was a strange sensation for Monsieur Labbé to be going through the city like this in company with the inspector. He needed to be natural, not to talk too much.

It was Pigeac who said:

"We may find she's back when we get there."

"It is perfectly possible. Except for what has happened during these last weeks, I wouldn't have bothered you."

"You did the right thing."

And that was that. Above all he mustn't feel uneasy. There were ninety chances in a hundred that things would go on just as simply. Yet when Monsieur Labbé saw Kachoudas' house from a distance, a thought came into his mind that worried him.

The little tailor wasn't there to see them, but his wife would very likely notice the two men. Had she got up? She couldn't have rested long. Resting isn't for people of that sort. Esther too might recognize Pigeac, whose photograph had appeared several times in the newspaper and who must have looked in at Prisunic at least once.

Suppose somebody said to Kachoudas:

"The inspector has just gone into the hatter's house. . . ."

He mustn't lose sight of the twenty-thousand-franc reward. Despite his fever, the little tailor would become anxious. Who knows? He might even decide to make the first move.

"Walk in, Inspector."

The heat immediately engulfed them. Monsieur Labbé was used to it, as he was to the half-darkness that reigned all through the house, and to the odors. Was the odor peculiar enough for Pigeac to begin sniffing disapprovingly?

"Valentin, my clerk. He got here at nine o'clock, as usual. He knows nothing."

Monsieur Pigeac moved forward, his hands in his pockets, his cigarette dangling from his lower lip.

"I take it you will want to see her room?"

Pigeac didn't commit himself either way, but followed the hatter up the spiral staircase.

"That is my wife's room, which she hasn't left for fifteen years."

Monsieur Labbé spoke in a low voice, and the inspector followed his example. It was odd: he looked just a trifle disgusted, as the hatter would have done if, for example, he'd been smelling the odors in Kachoudas' house.

"This way."

They went on down the hallway, and Monsieur Labbé opened the door of the maid's room.

"This is it. I could have put her on the third floor, where there are several large rooms empty, but the only way to get there is by an outside staircase, which would not have been practical."

The other man looked around self-importantly, and drew one hand from his pocket to open the clothes closet. He hadn't taken off his hat. He carelessly fin-

gered a dress the color of pink candy, a rather worn black velvet skirt, two white shirtwaists on hangers. On the closet floor there was a pair of freshly polished shoes, and on the rug at the foot of the bed a pair of shapeless slippers fit for the refuse bin.

"It seems she didn't take her things with her."

"As you see."

If only he opens the drawer in the bedside table and finds the photograph in the shellwork box!

He did so.

"Have you ever seen that young man around here?"

Monsieur Labbé pretended to examine the portrait carefully.

"I must say I really don't remember. No."

"Did you know that she had a sweetheart?"

"No. I paid very little attention to her. She was the uncommunicative type; in fact, rather sullen."

"I'll take this photograph with me."

He slipped it into his billfold, tried the key on the two suitcases, but it didn't fit either of them. Could it be the key to a wardrobe in Charron?

"Thank you, Monsieur Labbé."

He went downstairs. In the shop he stopped for a moment.

"I might do well to take a look in the kitchen. These girls stow their things almost anywhere."

At that time of day the dining room was darker than the rest of the house, and the inspector looked really disgusted.

"Is this it?" he asked as he entered the cubbyhole that served as the kitchen.

He found nothing.

"Will you take something to drink? I have some excellent white wine in the cellar."

"No, thank you."

He offered no observations. It was his way. Nor did

Monsieur Labbé. He was perfectly calm, perfectly natural.

"I take it I need not inform her family. You will see to that, won't you?"

"By the way, what's her family name?"

"Chapus. Louise Chapus."

He wrote the name in his notebook, which he fastened with a rubber band, then he buttoned up his overcoat before going out. Only poor Valentin was there to be impressed. When the glazed door had closed again, he watched the inspector walk away and asked:

"Does he think she was strangled?"

"He knows no more about it than we do."

A strange day. Everything was clear, bright, sparkling, yet there was something like a thin veil over people and things.

"Did Madame call?"

"No, sir."

He went upstairs, didn't even glance toward the bed under which the body still lay. He got to the window just at the moment when the doctor's gray automobile was stopping at the curb. Madame Kachoudas, who had heard it, ran down the staircase.

Esther was shaking her little brother, who was crying, and she kept pointing toward the back of the apartment, no doubt telling him that he mustn't make a noise because of their father.

The doctor's visit lasted a long time. Water was put on to boil in the kitchen, probably for an injection. While the doctor, after returning from the bedroom, talked to Madame Kachoudas, she sniffled and wiped her eyes with her handkerchief several times.

On his desk the hatter noticed the pages he had written the evening before; he hurriedly picked them up, tore them in two, and went to the fireplace to burn them.

Valentin, who lived with his mother rather a long way from the city, was in the habit of bringing his lunch in a tin box; he would heat his coffee in a little pot on the gas stove in the shop, and eat alone in the workroom, usually reading some sports magazine.

Monsieur Labbé wondered whether he should fix lunch for himself, finally decided to put on his hat and overcoat.

"I'll be back in three quarters of an hour."

He walked to the Place du Marché, where there were several small restaurants. He chose one to which the entrance was a step below the sidewalk and where the service was provided by a tall dark-haired girl in a white apron who knew all the regular customers. Among others, there were two or three employees from the town hall or the post office, a lawyer's clerk, an old maid who worked in a travel bureau.

He chose his table carefully, not just for that day but as if he expected to become a regular customer. The menu was written on a slate, and there was a varnished rack of pigeonholes for the steady patrons' napkins.

As a matter of fact, it was the first time in fifteen years that he'd eaten in a restaurant. The proprietor looked at him in some surprise and came to his table.

"What chance brings you here from your hat shop, sir?"

He might have forgotten his name, but he knew he was the hatter from the Rue du Minage.

"I'm without a maid today."

"Henriette!" the proprietor called, turning to the waitress.

He added:

"We have veal cutlets with sorrel sauce, and Burgundy snails at an extra charge."

"I'll take the snails."

It was a pleasant sensation. He felt as if he were floating. There was an airiness, a buoyancy inside him.

The people, the voices, the objects struck him as not being very real.

"A carafe of Beaujolais?"

"Yes, please."

"A carafe, Henriette!"

It was good. It was even very good. Louise's cooking had no taste. He almost ordered another dozen snails, and it wasn't till he got to the cheese that he remembered Mathilde was supposed to eat too.

"Tell me, Henriette . . ."

Everybody called the waitress by her Christian name.

"I want to take along a lunch for my wife. Have you some kind of a container?"

"I'll see."

She spoke to the proprietor. He vanished, came back with two small enameled pots which fitted into each other and had a handle.

"Will this do?"

Sunlight fell on the table. There were no tablecloths —or, more precisely, the tablecloths were of embossed paper and were changed for each customer; there was a basket in a corner where they were thrown away.

"Shall I give her snails too?"

Why not? He'd eat them. He walked home from the restaurant carrying the two pots by the handle. It was amusing.

"Has Madame called?"

"No, sir."

He went upstairs, threw away the cutlet, the bread, the fried potatoes, but he ate the snails without thinking for even an instant that Louise was still there. Besides, he preferred not to think about her because of the task that awaited him that evening.

In Kachoudas' shop the tailor's wife was explaining the situation to a customer, with despairing gestures. The customer appeared to be very much put out. He must have been promised his suit for that day, and it

wasn't ready; very likely it was one that could be seen, sleeveless and unlined, on the tailor's table.

Monsieur Labbé felt a little sleepy, but he did not sleep. He thought a great deal about Kachoudas as he worked on his hats. He missed his neighbor. Why, when he thought of him, did he have an odd feeling of injustice? Of an injustice that he himself, Monsieur Labbé, was committing. He would have liked to go to see him.

He felt that he could have reassured him, comforted him. He even had an idea in the back of his mind, and the idea was becoming increasingly definite.

Kachoudas, after all, had a right to the twenty-thousand-franc reward. He was seriously ill. He must be worried. What would his family do if he should die? His wife would have to go out to work as a household servant. And the four-year-old boy? And the girls, who got home from school at four o'clock?

Monsieur Labbé had money. He could withdraw twenty thousand francs from his bank account without running short, or use the bills that were in the old wallet upstairs.

How to go about giving Kachoudas the money was more difficult. Was it impossible? If he went across the street, he'd probably be left alone with him. He'd simply put the bills in the little tailor's hand.

It would be a fine thing to do. It was too late to go to the bank. He'd do it tomorrow morning. There'd be time to think it over between now and then.

An old pickup truck stopped in front of the hat shop. The driver, who was dressed like a village blacksmith, remained at the wheel, while a keen-eyed young-looking man with a drooping red mustache opened the shop door. Valentin went to meet him.

"I want to see the boss."

And when Monsieur Labbé came forward:

"I'm Louise's father."

He couldn't be much over forty. He'd been drinking, either at home or on the road, for his breath smelled of wine.

"It seems she just got up and left—is that it?"

So the police had already been to Charron. And the man had got one of his neighbors to drive him to the city.

"Did you keep her things?"

"They're still in her room."

"That's good. I've come for them."

He hadn't taken off his cap. He even spat on the floor, a stream of yellow saliva, for he chewed tobacco. He seemed to have come with hostile intentions, but the stillness of the house rather overawed him.

"So it's here she spent the week, is it? And she just got up and left without saying anything, did she?"

"Without a word," said Monsieur Labbé, showing his visitor to the staircase.

"Is it true that she had a boy friend?"

Since his voice was becoming threatening, Monsieur Labbé merely answered:

"She never talked to me about it. I didn't see him."

"Is it your lady who's an invalid?"

"Yes, it's my wife. I'll ask you not to speak too loudly; she's behind that door."

Nothing happened. The man piled Louise's things into the suitcases, and it was the hatter who handed him the shellwork box that was in the drawer. The peasant purposely walked as heavily as possible. Perhaps when he'd left Charron he had announced that they would see what they would see!

"Do you think the strangler got her?"

"I don't know. I didn't hear anything."

Despite himself he walked on tiptoe as he passed the door of Mathilde's room, and he almost fell on the spiral staircase, which was treacherous for anyone not used to it.

"Anyway, if she's ever found, don't expect her back. This is the last time I'll let one of my daughters work in the city."

He didn't say good-bye, merely touched his cap in a way that he tried to make insolent and that was only awkward; he knocked against the doorjamb with the suitcases, put them in the truck, and climbed up beside the driver.

The two men did not go back to Charron immediately, for the truck stopped at the corner of the street, directly in front of a small bar.

It was time to turn on the lights, go up to Mathilde's room to see if she needed anything, let down the blinds. The little girls across the street had just got home from school, and were being reminded every minute that they must speak in whispers. One of them was doing her homework, with her notebook on the tailor's table, which had been partly cleared off.

"I'll appreciate it if you will shut up the shop, Valentin."

The house was going to be left empty, and that had an odd effect on him; he felt a little afraid, as if something might happen there while he was away. He had no real reason any more to return at one hour rather than another. He would go to dine in the little restaurant where he'd eaten lunch.

If he'd felt like it, he could have gone to see a movie, but that wouldn't be wise.

Besides, he wanted to write again, but not in the tone he'd been using the evening before. He was less anxious, he felt a different kind of lucidity, and when, as he entered the Colonnes, his friend Paul looked up at him inquiringly, he was tempted to smile.

He didn't do it, of course. He had to assume a manner befitting the circumstances, for the news was already known.

He sat down without saying anything, prepared to

join in the game, immediately saw that Pigeac was at the table of the forty-to-fifty-year-olds, and at once got up to speak to him.

"Has she been found?" he asked.

"Nothing so far."

"You don't think that . . ."

Pigeac was playing cards and answered him absent-mindedly. The hatter already felt not quite so well. Not because of the inspector's being scarcely polite—it was affectation on his part—but because it was the dangerous hour.

It always began at nightfall, with the street lamps coming on, the footsteps that you heard on the pavement long before you saw a shadow on the sidewalk.

In his street there was a poorly illuminated window, with a dim greenish light, the sight of which had always caused him an indefinable uneasiness. It was difficult to analyze. It was sticky. Did that word mean anything?

The shop was a shoe store, and he had the impression that the people in it moved their lips without making a sound, like fish in a bowl.

At this hour the whole city was like that—a box whose lid had been shut. The people, no bigger than ants, moved about to no purpose.

Even in the light of the Café des Colonnes, it was agonizing. When he looked at the lusterless spherical lamp shades on the ceiling—there were five of them—he ended by feeling dizzy.

It was a little as if time had stopped, as if everything had stopped. The gestures, the voices, the noise of the saucers—all of that no longer meant anything. It was dead. It went on because of the momentum that had been built up, but it was going round and round in a vacuum.

That was what he would try to explain, instead of the confused sentences he had written the evening before.

Today he wouldn't let himself fall under the same

kind of spell. He was calm. He'd promised himself that he would be calm, would play the game through to the end, as if it were real.

It no longer irritated him, any more than it made him uneasy, to see Chantreau, the bearded doctor, observing him on the sly. What was making him stare at his hands? They weren't shaking. He had fine hands, white, smooth, with square fingertips and well-kept nails. He'd always been told so, even by Mathilde in the beginning.

"He must have thrown her into the canal," said Caillé, who was shuffling the cards. "They're going to drag it, but most likely the tide carried her out to sea."

"That would surprise me," muttered Chantreau, who seemed out of sorts.

"What would surprise you?"

"The canal. It doesn't fit in. Those people never change their technique. Unless . . ."

He fell silent. Caillé pressed him:

"Unless?"

"It's difficult to explain. Unless it's a different series, and doesn't have the same meaning."

"What meaning?"

"I don't know. Whose turn is it?"

In speaking as he did, he had avoided looking at the hatter, and the hatter blushed a little, for he had the feeling that Chantreau suspected him.

Why? Had he made some mistake? Was this sort of thing visible? Was he going to have to believe that the psychiatrist in Bordeaux was right?

Jeantet was back at his place near the window. He was writing feverishly, and from time to time a lock of his hair, which he wore long like an artist, fell over his face.

It was by her perfume that Monsieur Labbé knew that Mademoiselle Berthe had come in and sat down in her usual place. He made an effort not to look in her direction.

She had nothing to fear; he was in control of himself,

he hadn't brought his cello string. What had happened with Louise didn't count. He'd always loathed her. Finally he couldn't stand her presence any longer, and as for what had happened afterward, he scarcely remembered it.

"Two diamonds."

"As an opening bid?"

"I said two diamonds."

"I double them both."

That he would be going out for his meals changed everything. He didn't intend to hire a new housemaid. A cleaning woman would do, and not even every day, or if so, only for two hours, for example. If it hadn't been for what people would say, he'd rather get along without one entirely.

Julien Lambert's looking knowingly at Mademoiselle Berthe was getting on his nerves. Had he gone to see her that afternoon? Probably, for he was dressed more carefully than usual and he'd been to the barbershop; he smelled slightly of toilet water.

After three quarters of an hour the hatter had not yet finished drinking his first glass, and it pleased him, it gave him confidence.

They had succeeded—all of them, together with the newspapers—in making an impression on him. It was different now. There was no earthly reason why it should continue. All he needed to do was to be prudent, not so much in regard to the others as to himself.

Why was it precisely now, when he was being completely natural, even completely at his ease, that Chantreau should look at him so strangely? And something even more extraordinary and upsetting happened. At a certain moment the doctor played the wrong card, put down a club instead of a spade, which were trumps, though he had two spades in his hand. Arnould, who never forgave anyone else's mistakes, flew into a rage.

"What's got into you? What were you thinking of?"

Then, as if he really were being summoned back from a deep revery, Chantreau muttered:

"Of the poor wretch."

He must have drunk a lot that day, for he was in his sentimental mood.

"What poor wretch?"

Chantreau shrugged his shoulders, muttered:

"You know very well."

"The strangler?"

"Why not?"

"You feel sorry for him?"

He didn't answer, scowled, picked up his card from the table, and threw down the queen of spades.

For the second time that day—and both times because of the doctor—Monsieur Labbé felt himself blushing, and, to offset it, signaled to Gabriel to refill his glass.

9

Despite his big frame, there was something limp about him as, making his way slowly toward the café door, he stopped for a moment in front of the last table and looked gravely and appraisingly at the young man who was still writing and who raised his head when he saw a shadow fall across his paper. He was the one who had done him the most harm, with his idea of going to interview a psychiatrist in Bordeaux, and then with his tireless, obstinate, almost daily returning to the fellow's diagnosis to enlarge on it, to use it to explain the events of the evening before and to prophesy those of the day to come.

Jeantet hadn't done it on purpose. He was a child. There was no malice in him. Monsieur Labbé held nothing against him. Would it be his turn, forty years from now, to sit at the table between the columns, close to the stove?

They exchanged no words. They had nothing to say to each other. It was precisely those forty years that lay between them—perhaps nothing else, perhaps all sorts of things. The hatter gave a little sigh and reached for the door handle. Jeantet shrugged his shoulders and frowned, trying to recover the thread of what he'd been writing.

The reporter had begun it, and now his friend Paul was starting too. Had it been on purpose that he had spoken as he had? Did his words, which he seemed to utter without attributing any special importance to them, really represent a message?

Monsieur Labbé scarcely felt the cold. There was a

little more humidity in the atmosphere than there had been on the previous evenings—it was revealed by the house lights and the street lights, which seemed to shine through a blindfold.

Chantreau's two terrible words pursued him, weighed on his shoulders like paving stones he couldn't shake off, and yet they were apparently perfectly innocent words:

"Poor wretch!"

Jeantet too was an innocent young fellow, and he had given him the cruelest blow possible.

He didn't hold it against either of them. He held nothing against anybody. He walked along the right-hand sidewalk of the Rue du Minage, for he didn't need to get home; he was to go and eat dinner in the Place du Marché, in the same restaurant in which he'd lunched.

And suddenly there was something like a bright gap in the sidewalk some distance away, and as he approached it the hatter felt more and more anxious.

The door to the tailor's shop was open, and now he could distinguish two shadows outside it; he walked on, recognized the Spaniard who kept a fruit shop two houses farther on and someone who was probably his wife.

When he was quite close he heard a noise that sounded like the voice of a dog howling at the moon, stopped in the patch of light, and saw Madame Kachoudas collapsed on a chair in the middle of the shop.

It was she who was howling, staring straight in front of her, while the pork butcher's wife held her shoulders and tried to calm her.

At the foot of the staircase Esther stood shivering, with a shawl around her shoulders, for there was no heat in the shop. She was not crying and she said nothing. All that she showed was a sort of animal terror in her eyes.

Other people had come out of the nearby houses and

several of them were standing, motionless and absorbed, around Monsieur Labbé. A woman whom he did not recognize came downstairs with the little boy in her arms, though she could scarcely carry his weight.

"I'm taking him," she declared as she passed.

The bystanders drew back; she entered a house a few doors farther on. What had been done with the little girls? Had they been taken away too? Who was still upstairs?

The howling was as affecting as the harbor siren on foggy nights.

It couldn't have been long since it had happened, for there was the sound of a motor, an automobile stopped at the curb, the doctor hurriedly made his way through the group, looked at Madame Kachoudas for a moment, came back and shut the house door.

That was all. Kachoudas was dead. As soon as the door was shut, people began talking mournfully, and the hatter walked away, with the same feeling of injustice that had come over him a little earlier, when his friend Paul had muttered:

"Poor wretch!"

He no longer felt hungry. He could have gone home right away. He turned to look at his house, the enormous red top hat that hung over the show window, the lighted window on the second floor, with a motionless figure silhouetted against the blind.

It was then that it came to him that he would never set foot in it again, that he would doubtless never even see it again. He didn't admit it. To all appearances, he was the same as on other days, the same as he had been at the café a little earlier. Nothing had happened that could affect him personally.

Yet there was a lot to be done in his house that night. He didn't forget anything. He was well aware of the vile burden that waited for him under Mathilde's bed. He would have to go down to the cellar, shift the pile of coal

once again, dig, then, hardest of all, carry down the big heavy body. Wash the stairs clean, wash practically the entire house.

Chantreau hadn't spoken out, but Monsieur Labbé guessed what he was thinking.

"Here's the hatter again, as I live! I wager, sir, you've forgotten to bring back the containers. We have some excellent pork sausages with mashed potatoes this evening."

He smiled politely, found his place and sat down. The girl waited on him. There were fewer customers than there had been at noon. The room was almost empty. He was already regarded as a regular customer; she brought his napkin from one of the pigeonholes, as hotel clerks do the guests' keys.

He had declared in the newspaper that after the seventh it would be over and done with, maintaining— and honestly—that the seventh, like the ones before, had been indispensable. But the seventh had not been the real one. It had been an accident. It belonged to a different realm, a different series, only no one except himself, and perhaps Chantreau, suspected it. Or had Inspector Pigeac thought of it? In any case, Jeantet would think of it, sooner or later.

He would start from the idea that Louise's death was necessary to the murderer, "indispensable," as the hatter had written.

What conclusions would he draw from that?

But at bottom it mattered very little to him what other people thought. It was what he, Labbé, thought that counted.

Because of what had been happening at Kachoudas' house, he hadn't kept an eye on the street. He ought to have done so. Could Pigeac have posted a detective near the hat shop? Could it be that he was being followed?

It was certainly not unlikely, and as he ate he tried to see out through the windows of the little restaurant.

It was strange how tired he felt all of a sudden. Melancholy—that was the word for it. He was in the same sentimental mood as Chantreau at the end of the day, when he'd drunk a lot.

He thought of his house, felt bitter at the idea that he didn't dare enter it, would perhaps never enter it again. Why? What he'd done once he could do again. Was it because Louise had always aroused an unconquerable repugnance in him? Or because of Kachoudas?

He wanted to ask to be forgiven. Not by the maid. By the tailor. He was sorry he hadn't stopped in at the bank that afternoon. If he'd had the bills in his pocket he would have put them in an envelope and sent them to the family at once. If he went home, he'd send the money that was in the billfold, but he didn't really believe it.

The proprietor of the restaurant had no problems, no phantoms. He was pouring the heeltaps from bottles into a bottle of wine. It reminded Monsieur Labbé that he could have drunk, that he'd done it already and found that it calmed him for a moment.

All that was very far away. Things were moving fast. He was terrified to see how fast things were moving.

He called the waitress, paid, saw her put his napkin away in a pigeonhole, and it wrung his heart, for no reason. He gave her a big tip and she thanked him, surprised.

"Aren't you taking anything for your wife?"

"She's not hungry this evening."

"See you tomorrow, sir."

"See you tomorrow."

Patrols were on their rounds about the city, as on other evenings. He met one as he left the restaurant, and one of the men greeted him; he looked round to return the greeting, for his mind had been elsewhere, and he saw that they had turned and were looking at him.

Why? Was there anything odd in his appearance, in his behavior?

He tried to make out if he was being followed, walked toward the town hall, his senses alert, but could distinguish no sound of footsteps nearby. He passed by Madame Cujas' shop, which at that time of day was closed.

He didn't yet know where he was going. He realized perfectly well that he was likely to meet other patrols, that people, used to his regular schedule, would be surprised to run into him at a time when he was supposed to be in Mathilde's room.

He accepted the danger. More precisely, he scorned it. He had other things on his mind, or, rather, just one thing, and when, on reaching the quay, he turned to the left, it was clear to him what he had decided to do.

The doctor lived in a small house near the railroad station, on the other side of the canal. It was a narrow house, neither old nor new, very ugly, squeezed in between two others just like it.

As it happened, Monsieur Labbé had more than once found himself going to see his friend Paul in the evening—not as a friend though, but as a doctor, for he had always been anxious about his health. There was a screen in one corner of the office, and he remembered pressing his bare chest against the ice-cold panel while Chantreau put out the lights.

"Nothing at all, old man. With your physique you'll last a century."

After which they would drink a glass, two glasses, and Paul of course refused to let him pay for the visit.

He'd tell him whatever came into his head, that he had a stitch in his side, for example—which had been more or less the truth for the last few days. He might tell him about the sort of panic that sometimes took hold of his nerves, but that was more dangerous. From there

they'd proceed quite naturally to the events of the last
few weeks, to the man who was being hunted.

"Why did you call him a 'poor wretch'?"

It was playing with fire. Chantreau was clever enough
to guess. Hadn't he guessed already? He wouldn't dare
say anything.

If he'd talked about a poor wretch, it was because
there was an inevitability in his case, and that was just
what he wanted to make sure of.

Wasn't it the sum and substance of Jeantet's interview
with the psychiatrist too? He couldn't get rid of the idea.
Through all his comings and goings during the days
before, it had been with him, like a vague pain you don't
pay any attention to most of the time but which every
now and again becomes agonizing.

On the Quai Duperré, when the little tailor was still
alive and following him, he had suddenly understood
that the Bordeaux psychiatrist might be right after all.

In the darkness a fishing boat was getting ready to sail,
with a big acetylene light on the bridge, moving
silhouettes, bulky objects being shifted about. Behind
him there were two cafés, near the clock tower. They
were cafés of the same type as the Colonnes, with regular customers who came at regular hours, played cards or
backgammon or chess. Except that they weren't the
same groups. You belonged to one or the other. He
belonged to the Colonnes.

At the railroad station a train had steam up, the waiting room was only half lighted; taxis went by in the
street; might he be seen, be recognized in the glare from
the headlights?

He turned left. Then right, into the doctor's street, a
street inhabited by small tradespeople and workmen's
families. The corner house was occupied by a cooper and
the sidewalk was obstructed by barrels.

Chantreau's house was dark; bending down, he

looked through the keyhole and saw there was a light
burning on the other side of the glazed kitchen door at
the far end of the hall.

Well knowing that it was useless, he rang. The bell
hung on a piece of wire just behind the door. No one
could fail to hear it because of the silence of the house,
yet no one stirred.

It was eight in the evening. He rang again, saw a
shadow appear on the panes of the kitchen door, and
knew that it was Eugénie, the doctor's old housemaid.

The doctor had not got home, otherwise there would
be a light on upstairs or in his office on the ground floor.
Monsieur Labbé ought to have foreseen it. When he'd
left him earlier at the Colonnes, Paul had already drunk
a lot. On such occasions he didn't go home to dinner.
Out of a certain sense of dignity, he left the café in the
Place d'Armes and began going from one workmen's bar
to another, where there was no danger of running into
friends.

Eugénie had sat down again. She wasn't coming to
open the door. She wouldn't come. She was afraid too.
No doubt she was shaking. If he persisted, he wouldn't
put it beyond her to telephone the police.

A window was still open in a nearby house, and someone was looking out at him. He thought it best to leave,
and it was one of the most painful moments of his life.

Even Paul was abandoning him. It came to him to run
to the station. He still had time. He heard the locomo-
tive panting. It was the train for Paris, which would
leave in a few minutes. He had enough money with him
to buy a ticket.

And afterward? What was the use?

Kachoudas was dead, and it was perhaps the only
death of which he felt guilty.

The thought of Louise aroused nothing in him but
disgust. The memory of Mathilde and of the other
women left him calm, only made him want to discuss

them coldly, to prove that he'd been right, that he'd merely done what he had to do.

Why hadn't he gone to the bank, or brought the money from the billfold with him?

Just as he passed the canal he heard the footsteps of a patrol and, without thinking, he turned halfway round. He immediately realized that it was a mistake, but it was too late. If he started off in his original direction again, they'd wonder what he was doing.

The patrol was coming on faster. One of them tried to catch him in the beam from his flashlight but failed. He dived into a narrow street, almost broke into a run, walked more quickly, and still he heard footsteps; he even heard a voice saying:

"Where can he have got to?"

He was cowering in a dark corner. He knew it was absurd, but he couldn't help it. Luck was with him. The four men passed by within twenty yards of him without suspecting his hiding place, and ten minutes later he could start off again.

They were all against him, including Jeantet, including Paul Chantreau. They'd turned the city into a kind of trap, in which he was struggling.

He was really tired. He'd scarcely slept the night before. He couldn't go home.

He had gone round the end of the Rue Saint-Sauveur and, for a moment, he thought he was being followed.

Who knows if by this time Inspector Pigeac hadn't forced the door of the hat shop?

The first thing the police would want to do would be to go upstairs, enter the bedroom.

If Chantreau had been at home, he'd have had a chance to recover his self-possession. It wouldn't have taken much. If Kachoudas hadn't died, mightn't he have gone back to the Rue du Minage despite everything?

Two bad hours to get through, and, once Louise was in the cellar, it would be all over.

Above all, if Paul, when they'd been playing bridge a few hours ago, hadn't said that about "the poor wretch." Didn't that expression imply that there was no possible end to it?

He didn't hold it against any of them—not Kachoudas or the doctor or the inspector, who had behaved politely though coldly, not even Louise.

They were treating him very badly. They were tracking him like a wild beast. They weren't even leaving him a bed to lie down in.

They must certainly have posted a policeman near his house.

If they'd understood, they might perhaps have acted differently. But they couldn't understand, and he hadn't helped them. He had explained things very inadequately in his letters to the newspaper.

What would the clerks think if he went to a hotel and asked for a room?

Now every step he took in the city put him in danger, because he wasn't where he ought to have been, because everybody knew that where he'd normally be was at Mathilde's bedside.

Could he shout to them that there wasn't any Mathilde to look after now, that now he had a right to behave like anyone else?

He even had a right to go to the movies! There was a movie theater not far from where he was now. He saw its lights, the placards, he was aware of its warm breath. It had been so long since he'd gone to the cinema! He felt uncomfortable about approaching the little glassed-in ticket booth, holding out the price of admission. He knew the proprietor, who was a regular customer at the Colonnes, and he must be somewhere near the box office.

He was really tired. He would have liked to take a hot bath, lie down in a bed, between good clean sheets. He

would have liked to have someone, some gentle woman, lying beside him, talking to him affectionately.

Suddenly he thought of Mademoiselle Berthe, felt as if he were breathing in her perfume. He had already thought of her during the preceding days. He didn't remember just what he'd thought. Hadn't he almost brought the cello string with him?

If Paul was right, if the psychiatrist was right, there was no use struggling, but he didn't want to admit it, and he turned back, walked along the quays again.

He was staking everything; it was his last chance—he was conscious of that. It was a little before nine o'clock, and Chantreau might have had his fill. Who knows, he might find him at home. Even if he was drunk, it would save him. He didn't know what he'd say to him. It didn't matter. For fear of the patrols, he took a roundabout route. A policeman standing at a dark street corner looked after him for a moment. He must have recognized him.

There was no light on the second floor. Through the keyhole he saw the kitchen door again and rang.

After waiting for a moment, he left, and his manner was as wavering and irresolute as a drunkard's.

"Hello, Berthe."

He spoke in a low voice, with his hand shielding the mouthpiece of the telephone. The booth was cramped. Through the glass he could see the people at the bar. It was a small café at the end of the quay, not far from the fish market; he didn't remember ever having been there before, and most of the customers were fishermen. Mornings the women from the market came there to drink their coffee, baskets of shellfish were piled in the corners, and water trickled over the dark-red tile floor.

"Who is it?"

"Léon."

She called them all by their first names. It wasn't familiarity but, rather, a kind of respect, in any case of discretion. Never under any circumstances did she allow herself to address them intimately.

"What is it?"

He felt a little ashamed. His voice wasn't steady. He stammered:

"I'd like to stop in and see you for a moment."

"At this time of night?"

He imagined the warm room, the silks, the knick-knacks, the net curtains, the gold-tipped cigarette that she must be smoking.

"I'm so longing to see you!"

She gave a little laugh, murmured:

"It's impossible, my poor friend. I'm already in bed and I'm reading an amazing novel."

"I implore you."

"What's come over you all of a sudden?"

"I don't know. Do it for my sake."

He realized that she was hesitating. She wasn't one to be afraid, like the doctor's servant.

"I should have thought you'd be taking care of your wife."

"She's sleeping."

"And you've sneaked away like a schoolboy, have you? Where are you calling from?"

"From a café."

"So everyone will know you've called me."

"No. I'm in the booth. I'm whispering."

He was getting impatient. He could have gone down on his knees to her. He clung to the instrument as he would have clung to the doctor a little earlier.

"I promise I won't stay long."

What he wanted was to spend the whole night with her. The longing had come over him suddenly, when he'd first thought of her, her apartment, the big soft bed in which he'd never really gone to sleep.

"Listen, Berthe . . ."

"No, my friend. You're sweet as can be. You know I'm very fond of you. . . ."

It was true that she had always shown a special liking for him, perhaps because he was considerate, seemed to respect her, brought her flowers or little presents.

"You know my neighbors. They're well aware that I never receive anyone in the evening."

"Just this once!"

"Besides, I'm tired. If you only knew how pleasant it is for me to be all alone here in my bed, with a fascinating book!"

She was trying to pass it off lightly.

"Berthe!"

"There, there! Be good and go home to bed, and come to see me tomorrow afternoon."

She didn't understand any more than the others had. He didn't hold it against her any more than he did

against the others. It was terrible. She had no idea how terrible what she was saying was.

"I implore you!"

"I'm going to make a little confession to you and I'm sure you won't insist any longer. I've just finished getting ready for bed and I'm a sight with my make-up off, a layer of cold cream on my face, and my hair in curlers. That's the truth. And now you won't say another word."

"I'm going to ring your bell just the same."

"I won't let you in."

"Yes, you will."

"No."

"I'll force the door."

"Don't be nasty, my little hatter."

Perhaps she had been wrong to use that word. Yet she had used it without any irony, any malice. From her, it was more like an endearment.

"I'm coming."

She must have said no again just as he was hanging up, and he left the glass booth and went over to the bar, while the fishermen looked at him blankly.

He had to drink something, for you don't go into a bar to telephone without ordering a drink. There were two rows of bottles, and he looked at them hesitantly. One of them displayed a Negro's head. It was rum. He seldom drank it, except in a hot grog when he had the flu.

"Rum."

"A double?"

Why had everyone stopped talking? You'd have said that the people there, who after all knew nothing, understood the solemnity of the time that was passing.

They would be witnesses. And the men in the patrol he'd met too. And Eugénie, the doctor's servant, and then the unknown person who'd opened a window nearby when he'd rung the doorbell so persistently.

At such a time he was doing this or that. . . . At such a time he turned the corner of such a street. . . . At

such a time he heard footsteps and ran and hid in a dark corner. . . .

His comings and going would be traced. It was easy. It was the kind of work Pigeac was fit for.

There had been a moment when he'd given up, when he'd consciously begun to play a losing game. Had it been when he'd left the little restaurant? When he'd entered it? When, coming upon Madame Kachoudas howling funereally, instead of going home he'd gone on toward the Place du Marché?

Hadn't it been the evening before? Or perhaps the evening before that, when, with the little tailor, he'd stared at the door of the bishop's palace, waiting for Mother Sainte-Ursule to come out?

It didn't matter. He could have gone one last time to make sure that Chantreau wasn't at home, but it was a long way, and he'd run into other patrols. What would he say to him now?

Mademoiselle Berthe was expecting him. He was convinced that she'd finally let him in.

The rum was very strong. He felt ashamed to be drinking. The proprietor and the fishermen seemed to be watching his every movement.

No doubt the regular customers didn't stop at one glass, for the bartender hadn't let go of the bottle and was only waiting for a sign from him to pour again.

He gave the sign, not because he wanted any more to drink, but because it was the decent thing to do.

Chantreau might have come into the bar. It was places like this that he frequented in the evening. The hatter wished he would. It would have relieved him to see the door open and to recognize his friend Paul.

"How much?"

He paid, left a tip, but the proprietor called him back, and he felt embarrassed. He'd forgotten that in that sort of bar you don't tip.

He heard a voice:

"Good night!"

It wasn't meant ironically. He was outside. It was very dark. The moon had not risen. In the inner harbor, though there was no wind, rigging blocks could be heard creaking, for the incoming tide was raising the boats.

He owned a share in one of those boats, the *Belle Hélène.* Was it perhaps the one whose masts he saw silhouetted in black against the dark gray of the sky?

Someone passed close by, looked at him, turned round. It was a man he didn't know.

Another witness.

He passed under the archway in the tower, where there was light on the second floor in the little loophole-shaped window in the guard's lodging. The potted geranium must be in its usual place. He'd always seen a potted geranium at that window.

A policeman was standing in front of the Dames de France in the Rue du Palais. He had to pass in front of him. Why not?

The policeman knew him. They belonged to the same war veterans' club. He said:

"Good evening, Monsieur Labbé."

Didn't he know that the hatter ought to be at Mathilde's bedside? Everyone knew that. In a minute or two the policeman would remember it and wonder what had got into the hatter.

He was marking out his path through the city as clearly as Hop-o'-my-thumb with his pebbles, and it gave him a bitter satisfaction.

From the corner of the Rue Gargoulleau he made out the lights of the Café des Colonnes. At that hour Oscar, the proprietor, would be talking thickly, his eyes would be glassy, his gestures studied. Only the last foursome of regular customers would still be in the café. Before long the movie theater nearby would be letting out, with as big a crush as at the end of a High Mass, dark silhou-

ettes, people buttoning their overcoats, waiting for each other, women holding their husbands' arms, the sound of automobile motors starting, headlights coming on.

He could still have run into Chantreau. Or even Julien Lambert, or anyone at all. It might have relieved him to see Inspector Pigeac emerging from the darkness, even though he didn't like him. He didn't know exactly what he would have done, but he had the feeling that then it would have been all over.

If Kachoudas hadn't been ill, if Kachoudas wasn't dead, the little tailor would have gone on following him, and the hatter would only have had to wait for him, speak to him.

He hadn't much farther to go and his chances were steadily diminishing, were down almost to zero. If only Mademoiselle Berthe had been the sort of woman who would stay in her bed and let him ring in vain!

He was sure she'd come down. Not right away. She'd be angry at first.

The door to the courtyard was open. It wasn't closed until about eleven o'clock. There was a light on in the dentist's apartment, and music from a phonograph or a radio could be heard coming from the third-floor quarters of the archivist, who was a bachelor and often had gatherings of young people in his apartment.

He put out his hand. Why hadn't it occurred to her, after he'd telephoned, to go downstairs and disconnect the doorbell, as she so often did in the afternoon?

She hadn't thought of it. The bell sounded. She let him ring three times, then he heard a rustling on the stairs, a voice asking through the door:

"Who is it?"

"Léon."

"Be a good boy, Léon. Don't insist tonight."

"I beg you to let me in."

She turned the key in the lock and, with that, every-

thing had come full circle. She opened the door only a little way. She had on a lace cap over her curlers and a quilted dressing gown of pink satin.

"You're not being nice. You've never been like this."

He pushed the door open slowly, irresistibly, and all the time he never stopped hearing the music from the third floor. They were dancing up there. He could hear the soles of their shoes beating out the rhythm on the floor.

"Have you been drinking?"

"Only a glass of rum."

She wasn't uneasy, just astonished. As he'd foreseen, her ill-humor didn't last. It was more by way of being a game. She pretended to sulk. Her book lay open on the bedside table, which was lighted by a reading lamp. The lamp was in the form of a doll, and its full period dress shaded the light.

The archivist's guests danced on until one o'clock in the morning. When they left they made a lot of noise in the courtyard, and they had difficulty getting the door-keeper out of bed to open the courtyard door for them. During all this time they laughed. The laughter of the girls was shrill.

At half past seven, as usual, Geneviève, Mademoiselle Berthe's maid, who lived with her parents at Fétilly, arrived on her bicycle and left it in a corner of the courtyard, where there was a bicycle rack.

She had a key. She climbed the stairs and went directly into the kitchen. It was not until nine o'clock that she normally entered the bedroom with coffee and opened the curtains.

That morning she thought she heard an unusual sound. At half past eight, feeling uneasy though for no definite reason, she half opened the door and saw a man on the bed.

He was asleep. Mademoiselle Berthe was lying cross-wise on the rug.

Geneviève never even thought of going closer or telephoning. She turned and ran, dashed down the stair-case, gave the alarm to the doorkeeper, to the people in the street on their way to work. No one dared go upstairs until a police officer arrived, and they all stood staring silently up at the windows.

The policeman himself hesitated on the threshold of the room and took his revolver from the holster. He was a very young officer, his face covered with acne. He was a member of the soccer team. Behind him, the men were becoming threatening, the women urged them on, and Monsieur Labbé was seen to sit up on the edge of the bed, run his hands over his face, smooth back his hair.

Frightened for a moment by all these people, he blurted out:

"Don't hit me."

He had the presence of mind to add, pointing to the white telephone:

"Call the inspector."

No one could tell what he was thinking, what he was feeling. He looked at the rug, with a melancholy expres-sion on his face.

Perhaps things would have turned out differently if Pigeac, on his way to his office, had not happened to go through the Place d'Armes just then. People were hur-rying along in the sunlight. Gabriel was opening the door of the Café des Colonnes.

The inspector was seen coldly pushing back the crowd that was blocking the staircase amid mounting excite-ment. He appeared in the doorway, and the policeman got out of the way to let him pass.

He looked at Monsieur Labbé, who was still stitting on the edge of the bed. The hatter was fully dressed,

with his shoes on, his necktie undone, his coat rumpled.

The two men stared at each other, and Monsieur Labbé made an effort to stand up, opened his mouth, finally murmured:

"I'm the man."

The people on the landing who heard him claimed that he had spoken the words as if with relief and that when he held out his wrists for the inspector's handcuffs a timid smile had relaxed his features.

Later, on the staircase, when the crowd had finally been driven away, he had also said, very distinctly:

"Do not push me. Do not hit me. I am coming. . . ."